Praise for Kirsten McDougall:

'*The Invisible Rider* is charming, heart-wrenching and funny. McDougall imbues her book with a lovely optimism and an infectious affection for her characters; this is a writer to watch'
New Zealand Listener

'*The Invisible Rider*, Kirsten McDougall's first book, is such a good piece of writing that I am afraid of over-praising it'
Reid's Reader

Also by Kirsten McDougall

The Invisible Rider

TESS

Kirsten McDougall

Victoria University Press

VICTORIA UNIVERSITY PRESS
Victoria University of Wellington
PO Box 600 Wellington
vup.victoria.ac.nz

First published 2017

ISBN 9781776561001

A catalogue record is available at the National Library of New Zealand

Printed by Ligare

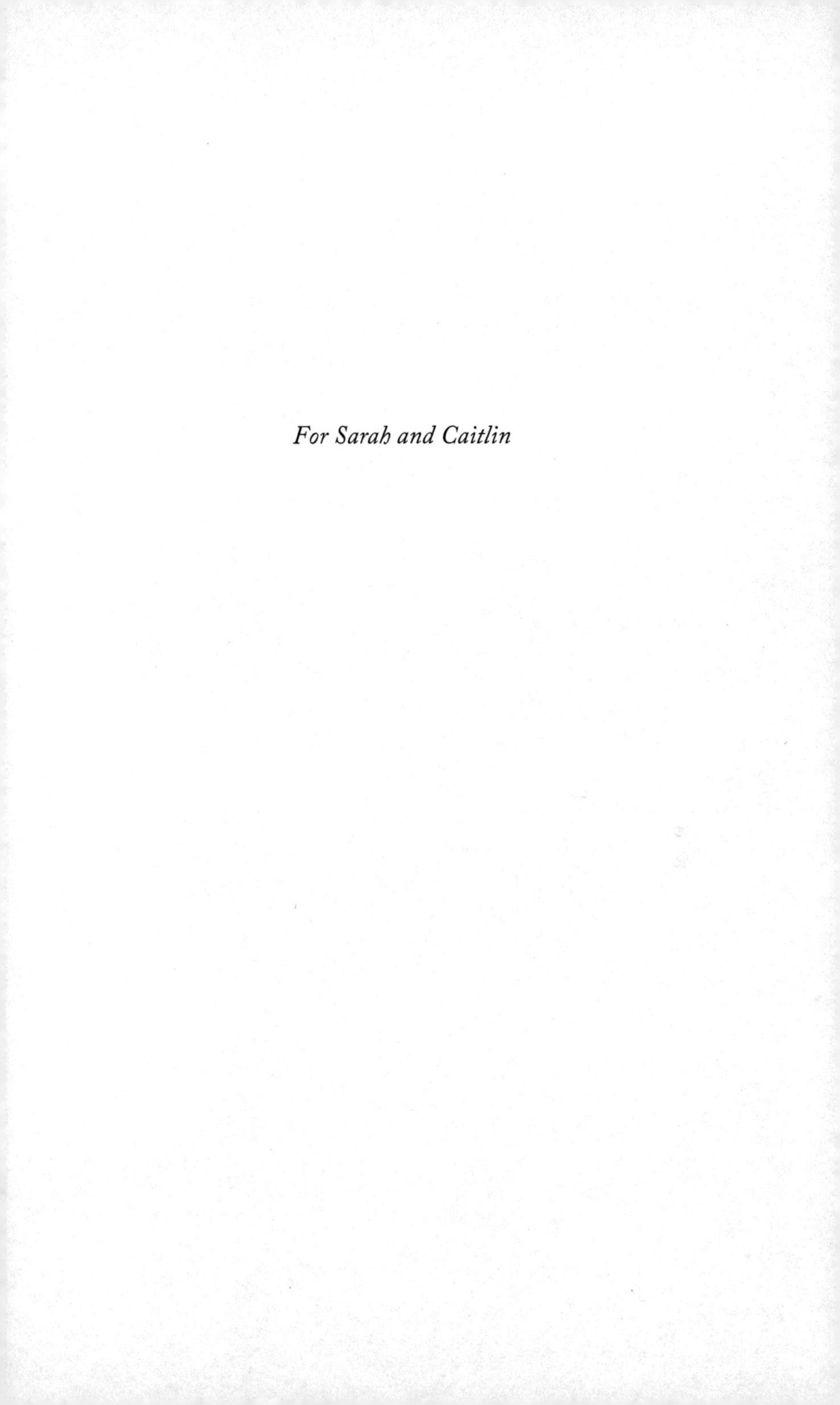

For Sarah and Caitlin

TESS

At first she was a blur of light and movement on the steaming road. The rain had stopped and the sun was breaking through the cloud in bright patches. Lewis wound down his window to let the stream of sweet fertile air pour over his face as he drove. His foot came off the accelerator and the car slowed as it topped the hill. That's when he saw her, moving through fresh light. She had a pack on her back and her hair hung in wet strings on her shoulders.

He could feel the car's weight, its urge to roll downhill and coast the straight, but he braked and changed down a gear, prepared to stop though she didn't have her thumb out. He let it roll, engine slowed to a walking pace. She walked on as if the car wasn't there, and he wasn't sure what to do. She either didn't want a ride or didn't want to risk a ride, even though she was soaking and in an hour or so it would be dark.

He accelerated and changed gear to drive away, but the car jerked to a halt and the engine stalled. He swore and hit the steering wheel. He'd spent hours on the clutch last summer. He'd fixed it. At least he could fix that.

The young woman was looking back at him. He gave a brief impatient smile. She didn't smile in return, and now the anger he'd contained all afternoon rose up and buzzed in his ear.

She walked over to the passenger window, pushed her hair behind her ears, bent down and looked in at him.

Her eyes were glassy and she stared hard. He felt she was

looking right through to the white noise of him, and his face flushed. She gave him nothing in return, only searched him as if she was reaching into his pockets, his ears, mouth, throat. He could feel the air pressure change.

Overwhelmed, he broke her gaze and stretched over to the passenger window and wound it down. She stepped back one pace.

'I was going to offer you a lift. And then I thought you didn't want one and then . . . problem with the gears. Where are you going?' he said.

'That way.' She tilted her head.

'I'm going to Masterton, if you want a lift.'

She looked south, gauging the distance, and clasped the edge of the door where the window was down. The rings on the three middle fingers of both hands were silver, turquoise, brass—junk found at market stalls. She peered in through the window.

He felt it as she looked—a pure intelligent animal intent—but he couldn't read her in return, could only be seen, and his skin bristled. It was as if she was below the surface of him, looking through him the way he'd search a water hole before diving in. Jean flashed before him, eyes glaring, mouth spitting names, the slam of the door and the long empty silence. He hadn't heard from his daughter in six months.

The young woman's rings drummed a light pattern on the passenger door.

'Sure.' There was a mountain ahead of them, and the road wound around it. 'I'm soaked through,' she said.

'My kids peed on these seats when they were little,' he said. 'But I cleaned it up.'

She didn't return his smile but she opened the car door and

got in. A fresh earth smell came with her. She put her pack at her feet.

'What's this car?' she said.

'A Mark IV Zephyr. 1970. I've worked on it, you know, over the years. I don't get to take it out much.'

She said nothing more, and sat looking straight out.

'You should do up your seatbelt,' he said. 'You know, for safety . . .' He heard himself as he pointed at the belt and knew he sounded uptight. *Why do you always talk like we're five?* Jean would say. *Because you act like you're five*, he'd reply. The girl clicked in the belt, then sat back in the same passive position. 'I'm Lewis, by the way. Lewis Rose.' He felt he should hold out his hand but he wasn't sure if she would take it.

'My mother's name was Rose,' she said.

She didn't offer her own name and he didn't feel he should ask. What was she? he wondered. Petty thief? Boyfriend trouble? Christian parents and pregnant? He started the engine and the car pulled away easy as if there was no problem. It picked up speed on the straight and he felt it glide over the road. A shaft of sun hit the mountain, and the green bush was lit and brilliant ahead of them.

'Look at that,' he said.

She nodded.

The mountain got closer and closer, and then they were on the winding road that had been cut in the side of it.

'Were you out in the rain the whole time?' he said.

'Yes.'

She was wearing jeans and a T-shirt, canvas shoes.

'You must be freezing.'

'I'm okay.'

'There's a rug, um . . .' He pointed behind and took one

hand off the steering wheel to reach under the seat. She moved forwards at the same time and his hand brushed her bare arm. She jumped. The car swerved. He sat up and steadied the wheel with both hands.

'Sorry,' he said. 'The rug . . .' Then he remembered the rifle.

She reached further beneath the seat. He felt her hesitate. The rifle was hidden under the rug. But she pulled the rug out anyway and wrapped it around her, no eye contact.

He thought to explain, then thought better. He remembered the times he'd hitched as a young man. The uncertain people you went with, being grateful when someone stopped and seemed normal. And being hungry.

'There's energy chocolate in the glove box,' he said. 'It might help warm you up.'

She nodded and found the chocolate. She opened the wrapper, snapped off two squares and ate them quickly.

'Want some?' She held the bar out to him.

'No. I had a big lunch.'

She didn't offer again and continued to eat the whole bar. When she finished she made a small satisfied noise.

'That was some rain,' she said.

'Spring rain. The farmers will be pleased. Although I don't know what it takes to please farmers. They only ever seem to moan about the weather, the government.'

'I guess you're not a farmer.'

'No. But I see a few of them in town when their teeth are sore. I'm a dentist. They're not so fond of me. Lots of them have bad teeth.'

'A dentist,' she said, as if she didn't believe him. 'Is that how you got this nice car?'

'Ah. No. I bought it for nothing when I was a student and

did it up myself. I used to do up cars in my spare time.'

'Mouths and engines,' she said.

He wasn't sure if she was teasing him. 'Yes,' he said.

In the silence she could hear the oncoming hum, like a large flock approaching. She didn't want to hear his story, she'd had enough of them. She turned away and kept her eyes on the view in front, though every now and then turned her head to peer out at the thick bush that lined the sides of the valley. The bush had its own peculiar language, unconcerned with human noise.

'I don't take this car out much. I've been to see my mother in Palmy today. She's in a rest home there.'

She looked down at her hands, fingers pale and wrinkly from the rain, and willed him to shut up. But she could feel it: he was desperate for company, for anyone. She looked back up at him.

'She's been there for four years now. It's nice enough. My mother's seventy-nine. Not so old, but she doesn't know who I am anymore. Today she called me a nice young man and asked me how my wife was.'

He didn't meet her gaze because there was the road and he was ashamed of how needy he sounded.

His mother was gone. She wasn't angry, as she had been when it had first come on, the rage that came with losing herself and the bearings in the town she'd lived in all her life, losing the names of her friends, of things. Now she was blank-faced Dorothy, staring Dorothy, who barely seemed to notice he was there. She'd been silent for two hours before she'd turned and said, *Where's your wife? The pretty one?*

'You staying in town?' He wanted the girl to stop staring now.

'Hm.'

'Family?' he said.

'Huh?

'Are you staying with family?'

'No.'

He tried to quell his frustration. This young woman didn't owe him anything. She hadn't even asked for the ride. And Dorothy, her mind was gone, that was the simple truth of it.

They drove out of the valley onto the plains. Neat grids of paddocks stretched out either side of them, their boundaries lined with tidy rows of eucalypts and macrocarpas, wire fences beneath them. Sheep and cows dotted the grass like a scattershot of ornaments. He felt the pleasure of the green wash over his eyes.

Lewis looked at his passenger. Her hair was pulled to one side, and he noticed her neck. It was long and slightly gawky, because she was still growing into her body, the skin youthful. He felt a pull in his groin and he turned away. He guessed she was his daughter's age.

'How old are you?'

Their eyes met and he saw her face pull into a scowl as if she'd seen his want. He composed an approximation of calm and turned his eyes on the road.

'Nineteen, if it matters.'

'Oh. It's just . . . my daughter Jean is around your age. She turned eighteen in October.' The twins turned eighteen and he didn't talk to either of them. 'It's a good age. Hannah and I married at twenty. I'll be forty-five in January. When I was your age forty-five seemed so old.'

'It still does.'

'Thanks. I was going to say, I don't feel any older, not really. It's just that everything in life seems to happen so quickly. You see,' he said, 'my wife is dead. I told my mother that three times today. *Hannah is dead, Mum, Hannah is dead.* And she just kept asking me where my wife was, over and over like a broken fucking record.'

She was quiet, but it seemed to him actively so now, giving his anger some space.

'Sorry. I know it's not her fault but I got angry at her and walked out. I'm still angry. But at least she won't remember any of it.'

'You remember.'

'Yes.'

'Then you should forgive yourself.'

'Oh. Well. I hadn't thought of that.'

She shrugged.

Outside, inch by inch, night was coming on. The sky had a streaked ruddy hue. Tomorrow will be fine, he thought, tomorrow will be a good day.

They drove the rest of the way in silence and it wasn't until Lewis reached the roundabout by the supermarket that he thought to ask her where she wanted to be dropped off. He was unsettled and his thoughts raced with the voice of his mother, of Hannah and Jean. People used words like brave and strong. He was neither. And forgiveness? That was one thing his will failed with. 'I need to go to the supermarket,' he said. 'But I can drop you anywhere you like. There's a hostel down the end of this road.'

'It's okay. I'll just get out when you stop.'

'It's no problem. It'll be dark soon.'

Lewis left it at that. Jean would get so angry when he worried that she be out alone after dark. *As if a woman walking alone after dark was asking for it*, she'd screamed at him. *In this town, she is!* he'd shouted back.

He parked the car by the supermarket. The young woman got out and hoisted her pack onto her back. Lewis pointed out the three blocks she'd need to walk to reach the hostel.

'I could draw you a map?' he said.

'No need.'

'Well, good luck.'

Lewis wanted to give her something or at least touch her arm. But she lifted her hand in a small wave, so he copied, and then she turned and walked away. He watched her move down the empty main street, deserted because it was a Sunday evening in early spring. The air felt damp already. It would be cold tonight. He walked across the carpark and entered the brutal fluorescence of the supermarket.

She did not like to take offerings from people. Not just strangers but anyone, and as she walked away from Lewis she chastised herself for eating his chocolate. To steal it would have been easier, more honest somehow. Now she would owe him for the bar and the ride and he would want something in return. That was how guys were.

But she'd run out of cash and the chocolate was the first thing she'd eaten that day. She'd stupidly put the bread she'd stolen in the top of her pack and the rain had gone through the paper bag it was stored in. Her fingers had sunk into the soggy paper loaf and she'd tossed it in the ditch. She couldn't eat that mash even in her hunger. It was a rookie's error to pack that way and she should know better.

From now on she would concentrate on simple things. Saving and storing her food, planning a way to the next meal. She'd thought there would be a paddock with a crop she could eat—spring carrots and early potatoes—but instead there were sheep and cows. If she could get close enough she could pull a teat of milk right into her bottle, it would be something to keep her going, but it seemed wrong somehow, to the cow, having a stranger steal milk from it.

She was aware that some switch had been tripped. There was an overload in her mind, distracting her from the few practical tasks she had to attend to in her day. She made herself think of the egg, of its simple oval shape and of containment within that perfect shape. And then she thought of eating an egg, of how good eggs were to eat and how her mind wouldn't stick to one thing anymore. She shivered at the idea of the night ahead. But she had to deal with now, with what was before her.

Shops lined either side of the street—a pharmacy, a stationer's, a coffee shop and a $2 Shop. They all looked run down, in need of a good scrub and a fresh coat of paint. The street was ugly, but it declared its status, not like Auckland where it'd been all shiny glass and polished metal which only showed you looking back at yourself.

The orange crumbs of someone's Saturday-night vomit were splattered on the window and tile wall of a Giftworld. Birds had been at where it had dribbled on the footpath. She gagged.

The man, Lewis, had been hard for her to see at first and she wondered why. What she had wanted was a day without the distraction of people, a day just to rest her mind on the green and the blurry white dots of sheep and the dark road bending away from her. And when he stopped his car she had wanted to ignore him, but she was wet and hungry and the road went on and on. When lonely men stopped on the road their intentions were clear. All of them wanted something but most of them didn't know how to ask for it or how to take it, which made them less dangerous than the ones who did.

He wasn't like that, that's why she'd got in his car. When she felt the rifle under the seat she thought she'd been wrong: that not seeing didn't mean safe, it meant he was clever. But he'd shown her enough. There was something about him she liked, despite his noise, his fear and sadness which seemed to have no end point. He tried to hide it, to be polite. People always thought they could hide their shit, but no one could, not her, not anyone. He'd been embarrassed by the gun, not defensive. But her own lack of concentration, just getting into his car like that bothered her. She wondered what was wrong with her, with her soggy loaf and her giving in and accepting the ride.

Still her feet carried her forwards. They ached. Her whole body ached now, and the rest she'd had in his car had only brought the sorry state of her feet into relief. The ball of her foot was wearing the sole thin on the left shoe. Her heels hurt and she could feel she had blisters on the knuckles of her toes. She'd heard someone say that climbing a mountain was just one foot after the other. But those people had money—you needed money to climb a mountain. They always skimmed over those details.

She heard the men before she saw them. They were half a block away, and when she heard their shouty, bored bravado she knew she should turn and walk away. But to do so would be to call them to her anyway, so she kept going.

There were four of them. One leaned against a wall, the others stood holding Tui cans and smoking. Three competing for the attention of the one who was leaning. He was holding court, nodding or laughing every now and then at one of their jokes. He was short and would be good-looking if he wasn't so mean-looking. He was sprung tight and his punches would weigh hard.

He raised his brow at her and nodded to his mates at the woman walking with a pack on her back towards them. The other three turned around and laughed, and their laughter made her empty stomach clench.

'Eh,' said one of them. 'Eh, girl! Where you going?' He sounded lazy, as if his mouth wouldn't open well enough.

'Shut up, Spud.'

The leader spoke as a farmer does to keep his dogs in line. He was still leaning back casual against the wall.

She should have crossed the road but she was so close now, just walking through them was as easy as walking off a cliff.

'Haven't seen you before.'

They were wasps, and simply by being there she'd upset the nest.

'Oh, come on. Can't you talk? Want a drink? It might loosen you up.'

They all laughed, and the one closest to her stepped forward and held his can out.

'What's wrong? Me and my mates, we're just having a drink, hanging. We're gonna play pool soon and Josh here is shit so I'm looking for a new partner.'

She was beside them now and could smell them, stale beer, sour sebum, oversweet scent of pot.

She kept moving, not fast but moving and not looking, and then she was past them with her back to them, which felt worse.

'Eh!'

She knew without turning that it was the leader calling out, and a cold fear filled her and she ran her finger over the loose metal shard she'd made on the middle ring of her right hand, her punching fist. She turned the shard so it sprang out when she curled her hand. She wouldn't look around until they forced her.

'My mates are trying to be friendly. Shit, girl! Didn't your mother tell you it's rude to walk away when someone's talking to you?'

A pressure on her pack spun her around. One of them pulling her back. She jerked away, making a yelping sound that embarrassed her. She should have been running now, but her pack weighed her down and she didn't want to dump what little she had.

The guy grabbed at her again and she tried to force him off, but he jumped back, out of reach. She was awkward and slow. The leader pushed off the wall and walked over to her. The other one had his arm on top of her pack so that she felt the weight of it pushing her down. The leader had his face up close to hers. His breath was hot, his eyes large.

'It's rude to walk away when someone's talking to you.'

She could see it well enough, the blank eye of a boy who has learned not to care. Nothing on the surface, just a cold silence because anything in him would be pushed down so far it was no longer part of him. They were most dangerous.

'All we wanted was to say hello.'

Her arms were still free, she could go for the eyes. Force the shard of metal into the jelly of the eyeball, run the metal along the bridge of the nose so it cut that too as it moved into the other eye. He deserved to go blind. But her intent betrayed her and he swung his arm around her neck in a lock, stopping her from swinging out, forcing her head down so all she could see was the concrete she stood on and the feet of the two others that closed in and she was caught. Still she brought her fist around as hard as she could, aiming for his stomach, genitals, any soft flesh she could connect with, but the ring had turned to the side and the blow she brought was nothing to cut with.

'You're a scrapper aren't you, you little bitch.'

One of them called his name, but he didn't let go and they called again, 'Let her go, Cody.'

Then she heard the car. She heard it stall abruptly and the door swing open and the feet of the other men move out of sight. The pressure went off her back and she straightened up.

Lewis stood on the road by where he'd stopped his car. He was pointing the rifle directly at Cody.

'What the fuck are you bastards doing?' Hard voice.

She sprang off the footpath and towards the boot of his car to put some distance between her and the men.

'Get in the car.' Lewis gestured at her but didn't take his eyes off them.

'Hey man, chill. It was nothing,' said Cody.

'Didn't look like that to me,' said Lewis.

Cody snorted. 'I didn't think they'd let you out with a gun.' The others laughed.

She opened the passenger door and got in the car.

Lewis cocked the rifle.

Cody held his hands up. 'Easy man, it was nothing. We're going, okay.'

'You were pinning her down, you prick. How is that nothing?'

'We're going. Come on, guys, we're going.'

'And keep the fuck away from my family!' Lewis shouted.

'What family?'

'I'm fucking warning you!'

'Lewis,' she said from inside the car, pleading.

Cody gave a laugh, then the group turned and walked away from Lewis, who kept his rifle on them until they were a good twenty metres clear. He got in the car, put the gun on the floor and started the engine. They drove past the men who looked but didn't start yelling until they were further away, their threats lost in the engine noise.

'Are you okay?'

Her heart hammered against her ribs and her T-shirt, which

was wet again with sweat. She was sitting now, but her legs still shook.

What was okay? Not dead? Not raped? The bar was pretty low. 'Kind of,' she said.

He reached down with one hand, pulled the rug loosely over the rifle and pushed it under the seat. 'It's actually only an air rifle, for target shooting. I mean it would hurt but it wouldn't do enough damage to those shitheads.'

He was shaking his head. He slammed his hands down on the steering wheel and gripped it for a few seconds.

'You don't have anywhere to stay, do you?'

She shook her head. She felt disconnected from the car and the sound of him speaking. Her body was back on the footpath, staring at the crack in the concrete where the leader forced her head down. She was preparing herself for whatever they would do next. She was taking herself out of herself so she wouldn't have to be there when they did it.

'Look. I have rooms to spare at my house. Rooms. Just take one.' He paused and then breathed out heavily. 'I don't mean you any harm.'

She was nodding and saying okay but it was as an automatic part of her. There were the nerves in her skin and the sweat that covered it but her mind had gone out the window, birdlike.

The car turned into a long, wide street that ran up a slight incline. Trees lined either side, their leaves light and new. Houses hid behind high fences. The car bumped over a railway line and the space between houses grew wider. Small plots appeared with a few animals grazing—horses, a goat. The car slowed down.

‘Here we are,’ he said.

Two massive pohutukawa hung like tall dark clouds above a high fenceline. The property could not be seen from the street, only guessed at. Lewis turned in at the open gate. A dog barked. The car wheels crunched over a gravel driveway that went up the side of a large lawn and the house.

It was grander than anything she’d seen in real life but not fancy. A deck wrapped the house on all sides, and a dog stood tall and alert at the back door, wagging its tail as the car approached.

‘That’s Toby. He’s friendly,’ said Lewis.

On the deck there were some chairs, a hanging seat in one corner, and it looked like a nice scene from a magazine where people might sit and talk or read books. Lewis stopped before a double garage and pressed a remote button on his sunshade. The garage door clanked and lifted, and he eased the car in and turned the engine off.

‘Right.’

He didn’t look at her, but got out of the car, opened the back door and took out the rifle. The dog rushed up to him and he patted it, talked to it in a soft voice. Then it came over to Tess and sniffed her legs and hands, wagging its tail. Its eyes were large and watery.

‘I’ll go lock this up first. Not that those chumps have a leg to stand on but it wasn’t the smartest thing I’ve done this week, wave a gun in the main road.’ He laughed to himself. ‘Let yourself in the back door. It’s unlocked.’

She got out of the car. Her legs felt weak and her T-shirt stuck to the cold sweat on her back. A security light turned on as she neared the house. She heard him call out from the garage. ‘If you want a shower, there’s a bathroom down the hall.

You could take the bedroom opposite that.'

She knew she stank. She hadn't had a proper wash for over a week.

Two boxed gardens sat either side of the steps that led up to the deck and the back door. She saw in the light they were tangled and bare, the sage gone woody, dead plants not replaced. She could help once she'd slept. There were ways to repay strangers. She turned the handle on the door and pushed it open. The light from the deck came on and she saw she was in a washroom. The smell of the house was musty and shut-up.

She felt for a light on the washroom wall and the next room lit up as well. Giant spoons and pots hung on metal hooks above the cooker; a fridge rattled and sighed. A mantel above an old fireplace held pictures of children, a blond girl and boy facing each other in a diptych, the woman who must have been his wife. The long sink bench had some dirty dishes. A large wooden dining table took up the centre of the room. A fruit bowl, a half-read newspaper. It was exactly what a kitchen should look like.

She walked over to the table and touched its surface. The wood was smooth, but bore the dents and discolouration of wear, scratches and scrapes where children had pressed down hard with a pencil, or a knife. She heard the dog patter in behind her, his nails clicking on the floorboards. He came up beside her and she put her other hand on his head and said, *Hello fella.* His fur was silky beneath her hand and she ran her other hand back and forth across the surface of the table, feeling the grit of toast crumbs, the grain of the wood. She felt and saw the world narrow in on her. All her senses came to the room where she stood, the dog under one hand, the table under another, and she thought it was herself returning. Then a harsh dissonant music rang in her ears, blotting out any other sound, blocking every other sense. Her sight reduced to a single point of light in front of her and then went blank. Her legs gave out beneath her and she crumpled to the ground.

When Tess was very young she went with her mother for a long walk in the country. They took a bus all morning and got out at the edge of a town where the houses stopped. They walked for hours, or so it seemed to Tess, up a long road. She did not like to walk so far and she complained and asked where they were going, but Rose just pointed out the plants you could eat and the ones you were never to touch—blackberry and puha, *Datura* and ragwort. She had stories for all the plants and the insects on them. There were kingdoms on the leaf of each plant, she told Tess. She squeezed Tess's hand, and Tess could feel the tremble in it steady just for a moment.

On this trip her mother carried a small brown suitcase with rusted silver clasps on the lid to hold it closed. The case still had Rose's name printed on it in fading red ink, and now it also said *Tess* in black, and her mother had packed it for her. *You get to go on a wee holiday*, she said. And when Tess asked where, Rose held her finger to her lips and said, *Shhh, it's a surprise.*

The day was overcast but bright with a light that hurt your eyes. Her mother wore large white-framed sunglasses and said that she should get Tess some—how nice they'd look together in their print dresses and sunglasses. Cars passed them and every now and then one would slow to see if they were lost, if they wanted a ride. Tess's mother would thank them and shake her head. Then they came to an intersection and walked down a metal road and didn't see another car again.

Tess looked down and saw that her legs and her mother's legs were growing dusty on the dirt road and her shoes were covered in a film of grey. Her suitcase banged against her mother's knee as she walked but Tess looked away from it.

Her mother pointed out a horse standing on the far side of a paddock, and they jumped over the ditch to stand at the fenceline and watch it. Her mother called out and the horse saw them looking and ambled over. Out of her handbag her mother pulled two apples that she'd stored there, gave one to Tess and waved the other at the horse.

'It's a chestnut,' her mother said, and Tess thought she was talking about the apple.

The horse came closer and her mother held the apple on a flat palm, offering it. Tess watched the horse turn its head to the side and open its big horse lips to show its teeth, which looked like old man's fingernails, large and yellowed. The horse wrapped its meaty tongue around the apple and pulled it into its mouth in one piece. It crunched down and small pieces of apple iced with long threads of white saliva fell from its mouth as it chewed. Her mother ran her hand over the long bone of its nose. It seemed to Tess that its face was mainly made up of its nose. Rose asked Tess if she wanted to do the same. Tess looked at the horse's eyes, large and shiny globes, and thought she did want to touch it, but then it spluttered from its nostrils and shook its head and Tess said no.

That was the first time she'd ever seen a horse in real life. She watched her mother touch the horse, how her hands pored over its nose and neck and how she leaned in and whispered things to it as if she herself knew horse, was horse.

Their walk led to a house sitting lonely in the middle of its own paddock. The house was shabby pink and though the grass was mown around it no attempt had been made at a garden. Rose stopped at the gate and turned to Tess. She looked at the old letterbox, which had no number on it and was rusting and leaning over so that if pushed it might fall. Tess shook her head.

'It's okay,' said her mother.

She held out her hand and her voice was soft, and Tess followed not because she thought it okay, but because she had no choice.

The door opened when they reached it, and Tess saw an old woman standing in the hallway. She peered down at Tess.

'Hi Mum,' said Tess's mother.

The old woman looked Rose up and down and then said, 'What have you been feeding her on. Air?'

The house smelt animalish and sweet.

When her mother had gone, the old woman sat down in a chair by the table. Tess felt a lump well up in her throat. A cat came and sat beside the woman, and the woman placed her hand on it, and said, *Good boy, Tama*, and the cat purred loudly. Tess wanted to cry, to call out to her mother, but she was scared of the old woman.

'So,' said the old woman. 'Do you want a cup of tea?'

Tess shook her head. Did she not know that children didn't drink tea?

'Well, I do, so put the kettle on.'

Tess got out of her chair and moved over to the kitchen bench, but couldn't see a jug to switch on. She looked around blankly, as if she couldn't even remember what a jug might look like. The Formica was peeling off at the edges of the bench and the top was covered in tea stains. Tess felt small and useless. The silence between her and the woman was heavy with the woman's judgement of her. She could feel tears welling and an ache in her body for her mother. Her chest was tight and it rose up high with her quick short breaths.

'What's your mother been doing with you aside from not feeding you properly?' said the woman. She grunted and stood up heavy out of her chair. 'Watch,' she said.

She pulled a dark pot off the stove and filled it with cold water. Then she took a match and turned a dial on the cooker and lit the match and held it to the cooker top. A flame burst out and lit the ring. The old woman put the pot on the flame.

'I don't keep the electrics turned on,' she said. 'Just gas, which they bring me in bottles. You never seen gas? Well, don't let it frighten you, but give it respect. Now come here.' The old woman held her hands out. 'I won't bite. Come on.'

Tess didn't want to touch her wrinkly old fingers, but she had no choice so she moved closer and let the old woman pick up her hands. She wouldn't look up at her, didn't want to see her old face. The animal smell of the house hung about the woman's hands.

'Look at me, child.'

There was a needling quality in the woman's voice, gentle but urging, that forced Tess to look up at her. She saw then that the woman's eyes were a faded blue and small milky flecks sat on the blue but the black circle of her eye grew large and concentrated as she looked straight at Tess.

'Your mother thinks you can see, but you look blind to me.'

Tess thought this yet another strange thing to say. Everything about the old woman, her house and her black pot and her fire to heat the pot, was strange and ancient. Did the old woman think she was blind because she couldn't see the gas or the stupid pot?

The woman kept staring at Tess with those big dark circles,

and Tess felt her cheeks heat up. She thought of a young girl, like herself, feeding a horse like the one she had just fed with her mother. Her mother. She felt a sharp shock of sadness and a tear escaped her eye and ran down her cheek. The old woman blinked and she looked disappointed. 'Hm,' she said like something was stuck in her throat.

Tess had heard what Rose said when she came back from the toilet. *Just for a few months while I get it together.* The old woman had made the same thinking growl. *Please Mum, help me.*

'Moss,' said Tess.

She had no idea where the name came from, only that it was the horse's name. That's what the girl like her called the horse.

The woman looked at her sharply.

'What did you say?'

'We fed a horse on the way. Moss. It ate an apple.'

'Moss died of a bad temper,' said the old woman. 'A bad temper and a bad investment, but still your mother loved him. She's always been good with animals.'

That was true, but her mother did not allow Tess to keep any, even a centipede or the pupae of a butterfly. Her mother always made her put them back in the garden. *It isn't fair*, her mother said. *They don't ask to be kept.*

'Did Rose tell you about Moss?' said the woman.

Tess shook her head. Her mother didn't talk about when she was little. Until now Tess hadn't even known Rose had a mother.

'Are you sure? How would you know about Moss if Rose didn't tell you?'

Out the window by the side of the house was an empty paddock. The long grass was being blown sideways in the wind, like a shiny mane of hair.

'It was just a name in my head,' said Tess.

She looked back at the old woman, who gave her a patient, satisfied look.

'So,' she said.

Tess looked around the kitchen to the funny old pot that was the woman's version of a jug steaming over the ring of fire. Something clicked into place. The gas made the fire. It was part of the flame. She nodded at the old woman.

'I can see the gas now,' she said. 'It's blue.'

'But you're none too bright,' said the woman. 'That much is obvious. Can you read yet?'

Tess shook her head. She liked the pictures, but the letters in the books made no sense to her.

'Hm. What about piano? Can you read your notes and play with both hands?'

'We don't have a piano,' said Tess.

'What happened to the piano?'

Tess stared at the old woman. The question was a test, like the kettle that was actually a pot.

'We don't have one.' She was defiant. Rose hadn't wanted the piano to go. When the men came and collected it, she cried.

The old woman shook her head and released Tess's hands and stood to attend to the boiling pot. 'You'll learn some basic chords while you're with me. And Tama and I will teach you how to make a proper cup of tea. What you looking at me like that for?'

'A cat can't teach a person how to make tea,' said Tess.

'This cat can, can't you, Tama?' The old woman looked at the cat, but the cat ignored her and continued purring, content in itself. 'And other than that, you can do what you like. A childhood's for playing in, that's what I say.'

Tess felt bold now, because the old woman was as stupid as her if she thought a cat could make a cup of tea, so she said, 'When is Rose coming back?' It was the first time Tess had used her mother's real name. It made her sound older than she felt. It side-stepped the ache that made her feel heavy and slow.

The old woman looked at her. 'Have you ever grown a carrot, Tess?'

Tess shook her head.

'I'll teach you then. It will fill in the time until Rose comes back.'

'When is my mummy coming back?'

She heard the old woman breathe in. 'I don't know,' she said. 'She needs to get well, and I don't know when that will be.' She sat down in the chair again and poured tea from the teapot into a cup with a chipped saucer. 'This teacup was Rose's when she was a girl. Would you like to use it?'

Tess nodded. She could feel her tears wanting to come back again and she swallowed hard against the lump in her throat. The old woman put two teaspoons of sugar in the cup and stirred it, then she pushed the teacup towards her.

'Drink it, it will help.'

'Am I going to live here?' she said.

The old woman nodded. 'Yes. And you can call me Sheila because that's my name.'

From the kitchen doorway, Lewis watched the young woman's legs fold beneath her. He rushed to her side. Toby barked and Lewis shushed him. He checked her pulse, which was beating fast, and also felt the hot damp of her skin. There was no colour in her face. Her body twitched as if in seizure and she groaned. He put a hand on her side and told her it was all right, all right. He waited for her body to calm, which it did. He told her he would go and get a blanket. Toby stayed with her.

When he came back, her eyes were blinking open. He knelt down and covered her with the blanket.

'I think you fainted,' he said. 'I'm pretty sure it's due to a fever.'

She murmured, and closed her eyes. He held out a thermometer. 'I'm going to put this under your tongue,' he said. He gently placed the glass rod in her mouth and held his hand under her chin to keep her mouth closed. When he took it out he saw the mercury sat just on 40.

He rinsed a cloth out under the cold tap and came back and laid it on her forehead. She shook as the cold touched her.

'Does it hurt?'

She nodded her head a little.

He went to the door of the pantry, opened it and pulled down the box he kept the medicines in. He found some codeine. A few years old, but it would do the trick for the pain. He took it to her and explained what it was. She nodded and he helped her sit up, take some water and the pill in her mouth. She lay back down.

'Can you walk?' he said.

She tried to sit up, but her head throbbed and she groaned and lay down again.

'I'll carry you then,' he said.

Very slowly he put one arm under her neck and the other under her legs and lifted her. She didn't weigh enough, he thought as he stood. She grumbled as he carried her through to the closest room, Jean's old room. He put her gently down on the bed and took off her shoes. He left her clothes alone. If she wanted them off she'd have to do it herself. He pulled a couple of blankets over her and thought to open the window. The night air was cool.

'I'll check on you in the night,' he said. 'Hopefully you'll sleep through. I'll get a doctor if you're still like this in the morning.'

Her eyelids were closed and he could see her eyeballs twitching beneath them.

'Okay?' he said, worried.

She moaned and rolled away from him.

He watched her for a few minutes, and, when he was convinced it was sleep rather than unconsciousness, he went back to the kitchen and poured himself a whisky. Toby padded through and sniffed at his food bowl. Lewis fed him and watched him eat. The dog always had an appetite. Sometimes Lewis wished he could trade places.

He stood in the doorway to the room before he went to bed. Toby was lying on the floor beside her, and raised his head from his paws to look at Lewis. The girl was still facing away from him, from the light in the hall, and didn't stir when he called out softly, 'Hey, how are you feeling?' He still didn't know her name. 'Don't die,' he whispered. *I can't deal with another body.* She was still but he could see the blankets covering her thin frame rise and fall. Toby yawned, then put his head down on his paws again. He was a dog who liked a vigil. 'Good boy,' said Lewis, then he turned the light out in the hall and walked down the other end to his room.

There was a girl on a swing and she was climbing higher and higher and Tess could feel the roll and pitch of the movement in her stomach and head, it was making her dizzy, and then it wasn't the swing anymore but men who were rocking her back and forth, pushing and pulling her as if she were a log or a piece of seaweed. Then her fear grew too great and she woke in the dark, sweating and disoriented. She sat up, her mind half in her oily blue dreams. She was burning. What was wrong with her? The day came back to her. The long walk through the rain. The ride in the car. Lewis holding a gun to the young men. In her dream they'd done what they wanted to do.

She touched her lower back and felt that her T-shirt was wet through. Her hair stuck to her neck with sweat. She quickly pulled the T-shirt over her head and undid her bra and threw them both on the ground. She lifted her hair up in a bunch and let the cool air calm the skin around her throat and neck. Her body felt hollow and achy. It's bad, she thought, and knew now it had been coming on for a day or two.

She wanted to stand up and open a window but her head was pounding with pain and she suddenly thought she might vomit, so she lay down again on the damp sheet and immediately felt chilled. She pulled the covers up. Her skin and muscles, even her bones were trembling with the fever and the hot-cold. She tried to focus, to hold her body still and make the nausea subside. She could smell herself, the sickness infecting the limp blankets and the pillow beneath her head, and she wondered if the bitter metal taste in her mouth was part of the rising stink of her?

Any good that was left was being overtaken by decay, by her own body's failure to keep what was bad at bay. It was as though she called darkness to her, like her blood contained the positives to all the world's negatives. She was afraid now and tried to call his name but it came out as a scratchy whisper, nothing anyone would ever hear.

Then she heard a whine and a movement beside her bed. A wet tongue licked her hand and she felt the dog's whiskers tickling her arm. She knew she must taste salty from sweat, but she also felt the dog was keeping her steady, keeping her still in her body. When he'd finished licking, she kept her hand on his head. 'Stay,' she said, and although her voice had no command, he did.

The sun was bright behind the gaps in the curtains when Lewis woke. He checked the clock and swore—he'd forgotten to set the alarm. In his mouth was a sour taste. His tongue felt sticky. He sat up and swung his legs out of bed, let his feet thump to the floor. His thighs looked pale, hairy and toneless. He thought of his father's legs in the hospital nightgown. Withered trunks. *That's what my legs will be one day.* Lewis kept telling himself to get more exercise. He groaned and stood, and only then did his mind flick to her, the girl in Jean's room. He pulled on his dressing gown and padded to the toilet. He pulled the door closed so she wouldn't have to listen to him piss. He'd not bothered pulling the door for six months. Jean hated it when any of them went with the toilet door open. *Men are disgusting.* That's what she'd said.

He walked into the doorway of Jean's room. The girl was lying on her side, facing him with her eyes half open. Toby was still beside her, but he sat up and shook his head. Lewis glanced to the floor, to her T-shirt and bra flung there, and quickly looked back to her. She blinked a few times, and gave him that wide-eyed look.

'How are you feeling?' he said.

She groaned. The sound was small and dry.

He walked over to the bed and picked up her glass. 'You need to drink water,' he said, and squatted down and held the glass to her. She lifted her head, and he held the water to her mouth and she drank a bit. He put his other hand on her forehead. She was still sweating, and her head was hot to touch.

‘I’m going to call a doctor,’ he said. ‘I’ve known him a long time. He’ll come here.’

She made a soft noise.

Lewis spoke quietly. ‘I don’t even know your name,’ he said.

‘Tess,’ she said. ‘Tess.’

At first he heard her saying tisk, tisk, telling him off.

He hadn’t spoken to Alan for a few months, but he asked if he’d come in on his way to work, not saying what for. Lewis led him through to where Tess was lying in Jean’s bed.

‘This is Tess,’ he said. ‘She collapsed last night.’

Alan looked at him the way Lewis expected him to, but he didn’t care. For all Alan’s judgements of people, he was still a good doctor—perhaps that was why he was a good doctor, because he’d spent his life weighing up the ways in which people’s bodies and minds failed them.

‘I’ll make coffee,’ said Lewis, and left the doctor to his work.

After ten minutes Alan came through and washed his hands in the kitchen sink. Then he stood watching as Lewis poured the coffee and handed him a mug.

‘I think it’s the flu,’ said Alan. ‘She has a high temperature. No rash, but you’ll need to keep an eye on her.’

Lewis nodded.

‘She needs someone monitoring her in case she gets worse.’

‘I’ve got no appointments today.’

Alan raised his eyebrows. ‘I thought things had picked up.’

‘Yeah.’

‘Is she a friend of Jean’s?’

Lewis shook his head and blew into his mug. The steam from his coffee rose into his eyes. It felt soothing.

'I picked her up hitching, dropped her off in town. Then I found her later. Some guys were hassling her right out on the main road.' He paused. Alan didn't need to know about the air rifle.

'Does she have family here?'

'I don't know.'

'Do you know who she is?'

'No, I just said . . . I picked her up hitching.'

'Maybe you should call the cops.'

'Because she was hitch-hiking?'

'You don't know where she's come from, who she is . . . she's sick in your house.' Alan shook his head.

'They were holding her down. They meant to hurt her. They only stopped when I—' Lewis stopped himself.

'What?'

'Oh, you know, I had to threaten them.' He shrugged like it was nothing. 'I knew one of them.' He changed tack. 'I went to visit Dorothy yesterday. I cleared some stuff out of her house on the way out of town. She's getting worse.'

'She won't get better.'

'No, of course she won't. I don't fucking expect her to get better.' Lewis jerked his hand in anger, and the coffee spilt over the side of the mug and onto his hand, burning. 'Fuck!'

'Cold water!' Alan's command was a bark. Lewis did as he was told, ran the cold water over his hand. Alan stood beside him. 'Hold it there.'

Lewis looked up at his old friend and could see Alan studying him. A small circle of pity rose in him, then fell away just as quickly. The pity wasn't for Alan, no. It was for himself. It was he and Alan who'd identified what remained of Hannah's face. Alan had vomited.

Things could have been so different. That's what he'd said after her funeral. They were both drunk and Lewis hated him then. He hated the implicit judgement, the blame in Alan's voice that he didn't try to hide.

Lewis lifted his hand out of the water and inspected the pink skin.

'Keep it there,' said Alan. 'So what are you going to do about the girl, Lewis?'

'Her name's Tess.' Lewis's voice was tight. 'Do you think she'll be all right?'

'You'll need to monitor her.'

'Please. Don't call the cops. I think she's just a kid who needs help.'

Alan's face was set, cold. 'You'll need to be here though, at least for a couple of days. She's too sick to be left alone. Have you got enough paracetamol?'

Lewis nodded. 'I gave her codeine last night. It seemed to help.'

'For Christ's sake, Lewis! You didn't know if she was fucked up on drugs or sick. Please don't take it upon yourself to do that again.'

'I'm not stupid,' said Lewis.

'Why do you act it then?' said Alan.

Lewis saw that he meant it as a joke. The things Alan meant.

'If my hand wasn't burnt I'd swing it at you.'

'You'd lose,' said Alan. He turned and sat down at the table. 'I'll write her a script. I can pick it up for you. No codeine though, unless I judge she needs it. And I judge she doesn't.'

Alan sat there scrawling across the pad. Lewis turned off the tap and held his hand up to inspect it. It was red but not blistered.

'I sincerely hope she doesn't cause you trouble.'

'She can barely move,' said Lewis.

'How's the hand?'

'Burnt.'

Alan stood up, his chair scraping the floor behind him. 'Say hi to Jean, when you're talking with her.'

Lewis had told no one but Anne, his receptionist, about the six months of nothing from Jean. He was ashamed, and Alan was the last person he'd want to admit the most recent failure of his life to. There was this swaying in him between worry and anger and shame. But Jean would be okay. He could only think of her out in the world making her way. She didn't need him. Jean would survive a nuclear winter.

Lewis walked Alan out. He held his burnt hand on the cool edge of the door.

'Put some aloe on it,' said Alan.

Lewis nodded and watched him walk out onto the deck. Because Alan's back was turned, he felt bold enough to ask, 'Has Lizzie caught up with Jean?'

Alan's youngest daughter and Jean had been best friends at school. They'd had a falling out, though Jean never said why.

Alan paused before turning around, and Lewis saw then that he knew what had happened—about why the girls fell out, about Jean leaving home and not calling. The ones talked about were always the last to know.

'Lizzie ran into her on the street.'

'Oh, when was that?' said Lewis.

'She told me Jean likes her job.'

There was something satisfied in Alan's face. Something that made Lewis want to drink.

'Yes,' said Lewis. 'Yes she does.'

Alan looked out onto the lawn and the trees surrounding it. 'You need a gardener, Lewis.'

Lewis nodded, then turned and shut the door.

The next few days were slow. Tess's fever burned on. Lewis brought her tea, water, cold flannels and painkillers. She ate a little soup, and barely spoke, and he didn't say much either, thinking she needed quiet. Toby lay on the floor beside her each night and was constantly pattering in and out of her room during the day. Lewis joked and said that the dog was her nurse. She seemed to like that.

In Tess's dreams Benny accused her of taking something of his. *Give it back,* he kept saying. *Give it back.* In her brief waking moments she was fearful that he'd been there, by her bedside, holding out his hand and demanding something of her—she thought it was the money. She told him it was gone, that it had been stolen from her. She sweated and slept and woke and slept and woke, and somewhere in the delirium Benny found her and she saw he had a knife in his hand. He came to her as if she were a patient laid out on a surgery table. *Hold still*, he said, and he took the knife and made an incision in the top of her forehead and removed a tiny round ball. *It's mine*, he told her and then he left.

When she woke she touched her forehead. There was no wound. But still she couldn't quite believe it was only a dream. It was a matter of waiting. Benny would come. He would find her.

Four days after she'd collapsed in his kitchen, Lewis saw her sitting up for the first time. She was staring out the window. He stopped by her door and she pointed to what she was looking at.

'There's a bird,' she said. 'It's making a nest in that ash tree. I've been watching it fly in and out all morning.'

He walked in and looked at her.

'You've got some colour in your cheeks.'

'I feel a bit better. Can you open the window?' she said. 'Your dog stinks.'

'So do you,' Lewis said, laughing. He opened the window.

'That's why he likes me,' she said, and smiled. Then her voice was quieter. 'Did anyone ask about me?' she said. 'While I was sick?'

'No.' Lewis turned around to her. 'Are you expecting someone?'

She shook her head. It still ached when she moved too quickly and she chastised herself because if she was properly well she wouldn't have asked him that, she wouldn't have said anything. But she wasn't ready to leave. She couldn't face the thought of walking again, of the road and the no food and the constant threat from men.

'Thank you for looking after me. I'd like to repay you somehow.'

'That's not necessary.'

'I don't have any money,' she said. 'I just have . . .' She pointed at her pack on the floor where he'd placed it four days ago. She signalled out the window. 'But I can garden. I don't mean to offend you, but from what I've seen your garden's a mess.'

'My wife was the gardener,' he said.

'I won't do anything much, just get it back in shape.'

'It's fine, you can do what you like.' He smiled at her and she smiled back. 'Actually, it's nice to have someone else in the house. Not that you've been very lively.'

She could see him better now. He was more open to her, perhaps relieved that she was well, and when she looked at him she could see his wife, the gardener. It wasn't a specific picture but a complex, cross-hatched patchwork of colliding images. His dead wife was like the tangle of convolvulus growing up the ash tree the bird was making its nest in. She would clear that first.

Wandering around the house two days later, Tess could see that Lewis didn't really clean. She was weak and her thoughts airy, but she could feel the illness receding and she didn't want to lie down any longer. Lewis had gone back to work. That morning, she did the dishes and vacuumed the kitchen floor and the hallway and her own room. She took the dirty sheets off her bed and washed them along with the towels in the bathroom.

She collected a cloth from under the kitchen sink and walked through to the living room for the first time. Toby, following her, jumped up onto one of the sofas and started to clean between his paws. The sun was coming through the window in a strong shaft of light, dust motes floating. The room was large, with a piano at one end, its lid closed. A dark leather sofa and two matching armchairs were arranged around a low, solid coffee table stacked with a pile of old *National Geographics*, some books with scenes of mountains and rivers. One inside wall had a large open fireplace, and on the other was a floor-to-ceiling bookshelf, custom-built to contain a stereo with a record player as well as books. Tess could imagine the family reading or playing games in here on a wet Sunday afternoon. In the winter the dog would be by the fire. That sort of house.

She walked over to the windows. There were cobwebs in the corners where the panes met the sills and she rubbed at them with her cloth, then lifted the sash. It gave a loud moan as it went up. She took her time as she wiped down all the surfaces, moving the rag over the bookshelves. She lifted up each photo frame on the piano, inspecting the faces in the photos. There were Jean and her brother as babies; there was a young Lewis in front of the Zephyr, looking proud. And there was Hannah, looking down at the baby in her arms and smiling the warmest, most personal smile. Hannah was beautiful, and her smile was quiet, joyful. Photos told a certain kind of truth.

After she'd finished these jobs she made herself a cup of tea and went out to sit in the morning sun on the deck. Toby followed and sat beside her. The sun warmed her and the dog was quiet company, and in the enormous overgrown garden something in her body let go. She could feel the rough painted wooden boards beneath her legs, her hands wrapped around the cup of tea, the birds flitting from one branch to the next. The garden in front of her was a total mess but it was better than all the concrete she'd been living amongst, where the only green that grew came through cracks and got sprayed with poison by the council every six months. Better than being surrounded by people who wanted something from her, people whose blackness threatened to swallow her up. People with no hope. They were the ones she had to look away from.

Tess put her cup down and stood up. She'd seen the tools in the garage the night she'd arrived. Gloves, loppers and a wheelbarrow—that was all she needed. She walked over to the side door. The day was bright, and when she opened it the contrast between the dark garage and the brightness rang like a gong in her head, temporarily blinding her.

Through the haze she saw the woman, a rope around her neck, hanging from the garage rafters.

She gasped and stepped back, slamming the door shut as she fell into white light of the day. Her heart was racing and she heard the buzzing, faint static that followed her waking from bad dreams. Tess was crouched down on the grass, her hands held over her eyes as if to block what was really in front of her, then the image passed and she realised she was rocking herself back and forth, trying to find some comfort. Toby came over and sat behind her, so when she rocked back she could feel him. She turned and put her hands on him.

In the garden everything was as it had been a moment before, peaceful and green with life. What Tess could see was attached to people. So either there was a woman hanged in the garage, or she was still sick and hallucinating.

She focused on the blue sky, the hundred different greens in the garden, her hands on the dog's back, soft and warm.

Tess forced herself back. The pulse in her ear thumped as she opened the garage door. The woman wasn't there. The bench on the other side was tidy, and the garage carried its ordinary smell of oil and motors, metal tools. Tess did not step over the threshold, but slowly closed the door and walked away.

She stood beneath the ash tree. It arced over her like a giant umbrella, its soft leaves at the top the only ones free of the convolvulus that was smothering it. She would do the work without gloves, even though it would wreck her hands; that was how she'd started out gardening, fingers in the soil, dirt rimming her nails. She wouldn't go back into that garage.

Working from halfway up the trunk, she started to pull at the convolvulus, ripping it away from the bark of the tree, and the physical feeling of tearing the vine off with her bare hands was good, separating the parasite from its host.

When other girls her age were reading *Sweet Valley High* and *Flowers in the Attic* and *Go Ask Alice*, Tess had been looking at the pictures in Sheila's gardening books. Together they'd transformed the raggedy old lawn behind the house into a place where potatoes and lettuces and tomatoes had thrived. At the A&P show, Tess had won a prize for the most unusual vegetable—an eggplant. Nobody in the district had ever grown one. The other gardeners had congratulated her but were puzzled by this strange girl who grew vegetables there was no use for.

Not Sheila. 'You have a gift,' she said. 'A real gift.'

Sheila liked to make the world seem mystical, but Tess knew gardening was the opposite of that. It was what she liked about it. She learned what the garden needed from her through slow observation. Seasons brought different demands, and she watched the proliferation of aphids in late summer, the dying away of the pests as the winter came on, curly leaf on peach trees in spring. She learned about companion planting, and about putting a sheet under the tomatoes so that when she squashed the stink bugs and all the other stink bugs played dead and fell to the ground she could capture them. Mostly, the garden wanted to be left alone. Feed it up with compost and leave it alone. In the garden she could lose herself, she could think about Rose and not feel sad. Sheila taught her the Latin names for the plants she tended, and she repeated them like a song in her own secret language: *Daucus carota*, *Allium*, *Lactuca sativa*, *Pisum sativum*, *Solanum tuberosum*. But her favourite crop, which bit and fought with her when she tried to collect it, needed no tending at all because it ran wild down the back paddock. *Rubus occidentalis*, blackberry.

Tess did what she always did when she gardened, she lost track of time. In her way Sheila had been right, but it was the garden that was a gift to Tess; it was a place where she could simply be. Toby barked and ran out to meet Lewis's car. She heard Lewis whistle in astonishment as he walked towards her.

'Christ,' he said. 'You did all this?'

They stood beside the enormous piles of weeds she'd made as she worked along from the ash tree almost to the back corner of the section. The hedging she'd cleared the weed away from looked bare and forlorn.

'It'll take a bit for this to come back, but it will. Did you know you had a row of daphne bushes in there?' said Tess.

Lewis nodded. 'Hannah loved them,' he said. He looked at her bare hands. 'You're not wearing gloves! There's a ton of gardening gear in the garage. You should have helped yourself.'

Tess wiped her brow. It was sticky with sweat and gritted with dirt. She held her arms out to inspect them. Beneath the grit she could see they were scratched up. She didn't want to mention the garage.

'It's so hot,' she said. 'The heat just grew and grew all afternoon. That's why I stayed on this side, for the shade.'

'Yep. It's unbearable by February here.' Lewis looked again at the work she'd done and shook his head, smiling. 'I was going to suggest the first swim of the season. There's a swimming hole up the road. Five-minute drive.'

Tess looked at him blankly.

'Come on! It's just what you need after working this hard.

I'll buy us fish and chips for dinner.'

'But I don't have any togs.'

'Oh, you can wear Jean's old ones, she's got loads of them. She used to swim competitively.'

Tess could see his pride in his daughter's abilities.

'Let's go.' He gestured to her as he walked away.

Tess looked around at the piles she'd made, and suddenly felt exhausted.

He took a track that led down to a bend in the river, Tess behind him, Toby at her side. The bush around them was dense and pulsing with birds and insects. Then the track opened up and they were on a shallow bank by the river, the ground bright and uneven with large boulders and small stones. From where she stood Tess could feel the heat radiating off the rocks. On the other side the bank rose steeply to hills that were covered in native bush and trees. The trees moved like they were breathing, giant lungs expanding and contracting, and the wind through them sounded like running water, imitating the river.

'Right.' Lewis pulled his T-shirt over his head. 'Straight in, no hesitating.'

His torso was pale and slender, his chest and stomach covered in curly greying hairs. He walked over to the river and went straight in, ducking under the surface. When he came up he gasped.

'It's good!' he said. Then he went under again and swam to the other side of the river, where he pulled himself up out of the water and onto a rock. Tess watched him dive off it into the water. He kept his body neat when he entered the water.

Her fear was outweighed by her desire to cool off, so Tess

walked in up to her knees. Within seconds the cold of it made the bones of her feet ache, and although her head still felt hot from the day of work she hugged her sides.

Lewis surfaced. 'Come on!'

She shook her head. 'Nice dive.'

'Thanks. I was a diver, once.'

He swam over to the rock, climbed out again and stood there, peering into the river. The water darkened his hair and held it close to his head, and for a brief moment she saw him as a young man with a fine-boned, innocent face. She moved further into the water until she was up to her thighs. The cold felt like a pure metal and she could feel her skin numbing. The water shone under the bright sun and the world was all surfaces and senses—the rough cry of cicadas, the rushing sound of the trees, the glittering light on the leaves, the fire of the sun radiating off the rocks and the icy river.

Tess watched Lewis climb higher up the rock. 'Will you dive from there?'

He didn't answer but stopped and looked down, then went onto a higher ledge.

'Can you see underneath?' she said.

She felt anxious. There was a boy in her school who had jumped from a bridge into water that was too shallow. He had cracked his neck and drowned. Lewis looked over to her and she saw what he remembered—a crowd of people, his own feet on the edge of the board, the still clear blue below him.

'Pike and single twist,' he called out to her.

He raised his arms and she watched him take the dive. His body curled tight and turned in the air. He was falling but somehow he was using his body to pull against the fall as if slowing gravity's force, twisting himself into another shape.

Then he suddenly straightened himself as his body cut the water.

Tess held her breath and waited for him surface. He didn't come up, and he didn't come up. She held her hand above her eyes to scan the place where he'd gone in but the sun reflected off the water and all she could see in it was the sky. Toby was behind her on the river bank, barking and barking.

'Lewis!' she called. 'Lewis!' She started to walk deeper into the pool. She went up to her chest. She could feel her feet losing their anchor on the river bed, her body wanting to float off in the current. She hadn't told him she couldn't swim.

'Lewis!' she called again, and then she lost her footing and went under, forgetting to move her arms and legs to keep afloat. She panicked. The cold water, tasting of minerals and leaves, entered her nose and mouth. Adrenaline flooded through her and her mind flashed black, and red and black. Lewis! She tried to shout his name again, but all it sounded like was bubbles and water entering her mouth.

Then she felt someone beneath her, an arm around her waist, and she was being lifted. Her head came above the surface again and she spluttered and took a gasp of air, then coughed and spat out some water. He dragged her to her feet in the shallows and she sat down on the rocks, coughing out more water.

'You're okay, you're okay,' he said. 'What were you doing?'

She was breathless. 'I thought you'd hit your head. You didn't come up.'

'I was just underwater. I like the quiet down there,' he said. He wiped the water on his brow. 'You can't swim?'

She shook her head.

'That's . . .' He stopped himself. 'Did no one ever teach you?'

She shook her head.

'You never went to the pool?'

'No.'

'Not even with school?'

'Um, I skipped those days.'

They were quiet a moment, then Lewis said, 'I could teach you, if you like. Not here, it's too cold. The town pool is better, quiet in the evenings. I used to teach swimming when I was studying. I taught Jean.'

'Uh-huh,' she said. She didn't know how to tell him, *I won't be here that long.*

The fish and chip shop was busy, and the other customers stared as they walked up to the counter to place their order. Tess's hair was dripping on her T-shirt, her shoulders were wet.

'Y'all right, Lewis.' The woman at the till said this as a statement rather than a question. She looked from Lewis to Tess and back to Lewis, waiting for him to introduce his companion. The woman's cheeks were made ruddy by broken capillaries, by hours over hot oil. Her thin blond hair escaped from its ponytail and stuck in sweaty strands to her forehead.

'I'm good, Jan,' said Lewis. 'How's business?'

'S'all right,' said Jan, looking at Tess. 'You got a visitor.' Her tone suggested nothing could or would ever surprise her.

Tess cleared her throat to say her name, but Lewis got there first.

'This is Tess,' he said loudly, like it was a full stop.

Jan grimaced and then nodded at Tess. When Tess turned from the counter, she saw a few heads switch quickly away. An old man who was sitting in the window called out Lewis's name and pointed at his jaw. Tess thought she saw Lewis roll his eyes slightly, but he walked over to him. She was relieved to sit down in the only spare chair. She picked up a well-worn woman's magazine and flicked through the pictures, happy to have an excuse to ignore the glances of the other customers.

The sun was going down when they got home, the changing light making a dense texture of the sky, like velvet.

'We'll sit on the deck,' said Lewis, then he disappeared inside. In a minute Tess heard music leak through the open living-room windows.

Lewis came out and handed her a beer. 'You cleaned the house as well?'

'A bit,' she said.

He beamed at her and sat down beside her on the edge of the deck. They ate the fish and chips out of the paper.

'When the kids were little we used to sit out here for meals all the time if the weather was good, playing records. They never wanted to sit at the table.' He sipped his beer, then said, 'It's nice having you here, Tess. I'm so used to my own company.'

'Everyone seemed to know you at the fish and chip shop.'

'Yep. One of the things about living here is everyone knows you. Knows all your business. Although I don't think Jan knew what to make of you.'

At Sheila's, people never came out to visit and she and Sheila never visited anyone. Except for occasional trips to the supermarket and the TAB, they kept themselves apart. Tess went to school, but the other children were distant, as if her difference was a smell. She knew people talked about them and she saw the way people looked at Sheila, their fear which sometimes presented itself as disgust.

'After Hannah died, my life became public property. People

either wanted to help, or they would just look at me like they suspected me of something.'

'Like what?'

'I don't know. Like I could have done more. Like I'd been careless.'

It was the first time he'd said anything about Hannah's death. Tess thought about the woman in the garage. 'Were you careless?' she said.

Lewis took another mouthful of beer and shrugged. 'Maybe. People want reasons for things happening, but sometimes there is no proper reason.'

'How did she die?'

'She was shot. The safety wasn't on. It was just . . .' His voiced trailed away. Tess saw Hannah missing one side of her face. The bullet had gone in above her right eye. 'An accident.'

She looked away and blinked fast. She wouldn't ask him more questions. She was not the people in town. The evening air was calm and warm, like a bath, and she held her arms out and raised them up and down in time to the music, as if she might wave away the nightmarish image.

'Where's home, Tess?' said Lewis.

It was the first real question he'd put to her since the night he picked her up.

'I grew up in the country,' she said. 'My mother died when I was fifteen, but I grew up with my grandmother anyway.'

'Oh,' he said. 'I'm sorry.'

'It's okay.' She shrugged.

'Where in the country were you?'

'East Coast,' she said.

She didn't want to name the town where Sheila was still, wheezing away in that grotty room. Tess couldn't go back there even though Sheila was the only other person she could trust with every inch of herself, the only person in the world who truly knew her. Every day she thought of things she'd like to ask Sheila. Like, who was the woman in the garage? Was that a memory or was she, Tess, going crazy?

'When I picked you up . . .' Lewis hesitated. 'Were in you trouble?'

She took a large gulp of beer. She could feel it in her knees, how it made them soft. That's where she always felt the effects of alcohol first. *You can't hold your booze*, is what Benny always told her.

She swung her legs a little, let her heels bang against the wood under the decking. 'I had an ex, I wanted to get away from him.'

'On the East Coast?'

'No. I was living in Auckland but I didn't like it.'

'Was he violent? Your ex?'

'No. Why?'

'You just seem a bit, I don't know how to say this politely, but you get this look in your face. Like you're scared.'

'So do you,' she said.

He laughed and said, 'Another beer?'

She nodded. He went inside and she heard him humming, opening the fridge door for the beer. Getting drunk was something she'd stopped doing when she was with Benny, but she was enjoying the feeling tonight. The sky was darkening above them, losing its grain as a few stars appeared.

Lewis sat down beside her again. 'So do you think the world is going to end, you know, on New Year's Eve?'

Everyone had been talking about it, about computers and dates and how planes would fall out of the sky. Mostly she ignored that stuff. She didn't bother with the news, and at the tree nursery she was outdoors most of the time. She'd never had a job at a desk with a computer.

'People talk about it like it's some sort of reckoning, like doomsday.'

'People are nuts,' said Tess.

'Yeah, you're right. We use a computer at work for our database, but Anne says she's got it sorted, so . . .' Lewis shrugged. 'I think I should care more than I do. I prefer machines I can understand, mechanical things. Anne tells me I should get a mobile phone too, that everyone is using them now.'

'Not me,' said Tess. 'They're expensive.'

He nodded. 'Do you have any resolutions?'

'For the new year?'

'Yeah, but it's a new millennium. That's kind of exciting in itself, isn't it? Like we should think big.'

'It's just a date.'

'For someone so young, you're rather cynical.'

'I'll grow out of it.' She gave him a smile. 'What are your wishes, Lewis?'

He took a while to answer. 'I think I'd like to stop being a dentist. Gosh. That's the first time I've said that out loud.'

'What would you do?'

'I don't know. I like working on cars, building stuff. What else is there? I guess I'd just like to have a sense of possibility. Of there being more than this.' He held his arms up.

'This is pretty nice,' she said.

'Yeah,' he said. 'But I guess I'd like to be with someone, to share my life with someone. It gets lonely by yourself.'

Tess thought of the woman in the garage. Having her was

worse than being alone.

'What about you, Tess? Do you have any things you want for your future?'

Tess found it hard to think ahead. How did all those other people do it? All those people living normal lives like Lewis's. Did they plan them out? Go to university or get a job and save up money and buy a house. She couldn't see how she could be a part of that world, although the idea of staying in one place, having her own garden, with little interruption from the outside, was a nice one. It was how Sheila had lived for a long time, until she got sick.

Tess should've been with her. If she'd been good, she would have stayed.

When Benny took the knife to Doug's thigh, Tess had shouted, *Mind the artery!*

Mind the artery, but Benny's grip was tight around the knife and when he looked up at her she knew to be quiet or he would do worse.

He had promised. Benny had promised he'd only hurt Doug enough to get the money. But Tess had seen the look in him, murk. It was pitiless and it was impossible to tell where Benny's limits were. She'd seen it before, when he hit her. Afterwards, he'd cry, saying, *Sorry sorry I'm so sorry I love you*, and he was sorry and maybe he did love her. So she forgave him because she could see how it came over him like a thick fog sealing him in, making him blind.

And now there was a gash in Doug's jeans and the spreading blood was a dark patch on the denim. The colour in Doug's face had run down into his leg. His mouth was going open shut open shut like a fish. He'd already given them the money, but Benny had to hurt him for what he'd done, and when he put the knife in again it was as if he was stabbing someone only he could see. Tess thought of it as a nebulous form, a memory he'd turned into his constant shadow, his monster, the place where his rage fed.

Over the next two weeks Lewis took her to the town pool. They went in the early evening when there was a lull while most people were at home eating dinner. Later, when the swimming squads arrived for training, they'd leave. Lewis stood in the water at the shallow end with her and made her float along with a board held between her arms. At first the feeling of holding herself up in the water was strange and she felt how her legs kept sinking. She felt that it was something she'd never be able to do.

'You're forgetting to kick,' he said. 'Of course you'll sink if you don't kick.'

He held her legs and moved them in the water for her while she held on to the board. It felt odd, having someone manipulate her legs like that. But then she tried it herself and it worked. By moving her legs and feet she could propel herself forwards. Lewis showed her to push herself off from the wall to give herself some momentum. He cheered when she kicked with the board halfway down the length of the pool. The effort made Tess tired, but then she kicked back to him. He was smiling right across his face.

Then one night Lewis said she had to put her face in the water.

'But I can't breathe,' she said. 'I don't know how breathe with my face under.'

'You're not a fish!' he said. 'You breathe out underwater and then you bring your head up again to breathe in.'

Tess laughed at her mistake. And when he said, 'Are you

ready?' she put her face into the water. It felt terrible, like suffocating, and she came up and spluttered. She felt like kicking him, except he was too patient, too kind.

'You just need to practise,' he said.

He showed her what he wanted her to do, then he held her head gently and showed her how to turn it one way and breathe in, head down and breathe out, then head to the other side and breathe in again. His hand on the back of her head was firm, but it felt safe. She could see how much he was enjoying teaching her. After a few nights she managed to float with the board and breathe and remember to kick. It was a lot to remember to do at once. But Tess felt good. Lying in bed at night she imagined herself kicking and breathing, kicking and breathing. As she dissolved into sleep she could feel the motion of the water against her as if her body were a boat, her arms and legs its oars.

Her days started to have a rhythm to them—gardening in the day with Toby at her side, swimming lessons in the early evening. After her lesson they'd eat something she'd made, sitting either at the kitchen table or out on the deck. Lewis said she didn't need to cook every night, but she wanted to. By two in the afternoon it was too hot to be outside anyway. She'd come in and read for couple of hours, then prepare a meal.

The heat seemed to build each day and Tess watched as the grass slowly turned brown.

'This is what the summer is like here,' said Lewis. 'Hot and dry. It'll be a fire hazard by February, but your vegetables will be growing like crazy if you water them.'

For once Tess didn't stop to think she wouldn't be here to see the crop. Each day she stayed, it got harder to leave. She could feel herself attaching, the fine threads of roots spreading out. If she kept her eyes averted she could get carried along on the day's rhythm. Even her dreams left her alone, and when she woke each morning she no longer wondered where she was. Her bearings felt solid as she remembered the room, the house, the garden outside, the sound of Lewis bumping around in the kitchen before he left for work.

At the pool she was learning to enjoy being under the water. She told Lewis one night she wanted him to teach her how to swim along the bottom of the pool.

'You'll have to learn to move your arms then,' he said.

They'd finished eating and he pushed his chair back from the table. 'You should practise the movement out of the water. It's good for your muscle memory.' He stood up and showed her how, moving his arms in large circles in front of him.

Tess copied him.

'That's it,' he said. 'But you need to put some reach into it.' He stood behind her and held her arms, moving them in circles for her, instructing her to keep her fingers together, like paddles, to catch the water. He'd touched her in the water like this, manipulating her body to show her how to place it in the water, but in the room it felt different, his hands on her bare arms, guiding them.

Tess felt the dreamy mood she'd allowed herself to fall back into, as if she were already on the pool floor, looking around at the watery, slow-moving world. Lewis stopped moving her arms and leaned down and kissed her on the neck. She froze, uncertain what was happening. Then he bent her around towards him and looked at her questioningly. But she saw what was in his eyes—not her but another woman. She pushed him away and stumbled back.

'Tess?' he said. 'I'm sorry, I shouldn't have . . .'

'I'm not . . .' she said. She was still underwater, unable to breathe. It didn't feel right. It was the same feeling she'd always had when a guy tried to kiss her: numb.

'What?' he said.

'I'm not into you, not like . . .' she said. Her voice sounded harsh. She softened it. 'Anyway, you were thinking of someone else.' As soon as she said it, she wished she could take it back.

'No, I . . .'

'Don't lie.'

He sank back down in his chair and put his head in his hands. 'I'm sorry. I shouldn't have done that. I just . . . I didn't think.'

Without coming closer to him, she leaned forward and picked her plate off the table. She held her other hand out. 'Pass me your plate.'

'You don't have to do the dishes. You don't have to do any of this work. I don't expect it.'

She didn't answer him but kept holding her hand out until he gave her his plate. Behind her she heard him stand and walk out of the room, out onto the deck. She heard his footsteps on the gravel and she guessed he was going out to the garage. She filled the basin with water and started to wash the dishes. The water was too hot, but she kept her hands in it because the scalding on her skin distracted her.

It was what she hated most, watching people lie. She couldn't always see it. Sometimes, when she realised later that someone had lied to her, she liked that she hadn't seen it, that she'd had to rely on her instincts the way everyone else did. Lately, her instincts hadn't been that reliable. Benny was full of lies. His lies were tangled up in knots that he couldn't untie. That's why she couldn't hate him. Not even after what happened. Why, though, was Lewis trying to kiss her? She'd begun to trust him and feel safe here. Was there nowhere she could relax? And she'd promised herself during all those days walking after she left Benny that she would only get close to people who felt true and right. Lewis had felt like that, but she'd been wrong. If only she could take people at face value. Sometimes it was unbearable this thing she could do.

When she finished the dishes she made a cup of tea and sat down at the kitchen table. She would wait here until he came back. She picked up the book she'd been reading, a children's novel about some kids on an island trying to find an ox carved out of gold. The adults in it were bad. She'd found a stash of children's books in Jonathan's room when she was cleaning the house. One afternoon she'd lain down on the bed in that room and started a book about a boy who finds a caveman living in a chalk cave near his house. She liked the way the children in it were smart and the adults were mean and dumb. She liked being in Jonathan's room also. It was darker and cooler than Jean's, and the curtains had characters from *The Empire Strikes Back*, which was the only movie she and Rose ever saw at the cinema together. This was where she came in the afternoons to read, and it comforted her.

But now at the table she could hardly focus on the words as they ran and blurred before her eyes. She must have been staring at the page for half an hour before Lewis came back in again. He paused in the doorway and looked at her, his face calm. He came over to the table and sat down opposite her.

'I'm sorry,' he said. 'I shouldn't have tried to kiss you. I don't know what came over me. I like you being here and you should stay for as long as you need to.'

She was silent. He wasn't going to get away with it that easily.

'I'm old enough to be your father.' He paused. 'God, that sounds awful.' He put his head in his hands and looked down at the table.

Tess turned to him. The sadness had been there in Lewis from when they met and now she saw it clearly, the part of him that he was no longer hiding from her. The grief he carried had burrowed in under his skin and fixed itself to his bones—that's how she saw it now, as part of his body affecting the way he moved and thought and acted and slept. There was no way to distinguish him from it. It got into her, got beneath her resolve to punish him. She wanted to give him something.

She spoke slowly. 'I left someone in Auckland . . . I guess I'm still getting over him.' She trailed off because she didn't know how to match Lewis's openness, nor how to talk about the knot of yearning and confusion she felt inside. Benny was the only boyfriend she'd had and she'd just allowed it to happen when she should have walked away. The idea that they'd ever slept together made her feel ill. What he'd offered was a temporary place to stay. What Tess wanted was a home. She didn't care about Benny. Leaving him was relief.

He nodded. Perhaps there were things that people didn't need to say; perhaps it was all in the way you stood, the tone of your voice. There was what people said and what they thought, two different things. She couldn't absorb it all.

'There's something I don't quite understand,' he said.

She rubbed her finger on the book's edge, which was soft and rounded with wear. She knew what he was going to ask but she'd wait for him to ask it. She had no idea what she should say. *You must never ever tell anyone.* That's what Sheila had said. She'd told Benny, and look what had happened.

'About what?' She kept her eyes on the book.

'You said I was thinking of someone else, and you were right. I didn't think I was, but . . . I was. How did you know? I didn't, ah, I didn't say her name, did I?'

His cheeks reddened. Tess felt the spool inside her unravel a little more. She could lie. She could say he gave himself away.

'No, you didn't.' Her voice was quiet but firm, and she was surprised by this, the confidence of her negation. 'She has brown hair and a mole on her cheek—' Tess pointed at her own cheek '—here below her eye. She wears a white coat. She looks very clean and you like her a lot.'

He was looking at her now, his eyes wide, taking in everything she said.

'Nicky,' he said softly.

'Nicky,' said Tess.

'I worked with her. She was my dental assistant. We . . .' He was running his fingers over the surface of the table now. 'How did you know?' He looked around the room as if searching for clues. His tone became accusatory. 'What have you been doing while I'm at work?'

Tess's anger flared. She hated people thinking that she was a sneak, going into their cupboards and drawers, finding out all their secrets. She didn't need more than she had seen in him. She could guess the rest.

'You were with her when Hannah died, weren't you?' she said. 'That's why you're alone in this house.'

He looked up sharply and jerked his head back, wary. 'Who are you?'

She could see he was hurting, but his eyes were clear. His question poked at the truth of her better than most people could manage, most people who had ever accused her of being strange. It was genuine. Who was she?

'I'm no one,' she said.

'You're not no one.' He gave a frustrated sigh. 'But I barely know anything about you and you seem to know a lot about me. Has Alan been around? Is that how you know about Nicky?'

The reel that had been unwinding in Tess for weeks now came to the end of its thread. She couldn't lie to this man anymore. Not because she owed him or she felt that he wanted something from her, but because he didn't.

'I can see things in people.' She glanced up at him as she said it, to see if he was judging her, but he was listening, and patient, so she continued. 'When people talk they remember stuff. If a memory is vivid enough in someone, I can see it. When you kissed me you were remembering your friend.'

His face was still, taking in what she had said. He was not trying to deny what she was and neither did he look disgusted, which was what Benny's first reaction had been.

All she could see was some sort of shifting emotion in Lewis's face, like a cloud making shapes over a landscape, as he tried to understand what she was telling him.

He paused, weighing his words. 'The way you look at me sometimes. Like you're looking through me.'

Tess blinked like she wanted to cry. There was something sharp in her, and the cutting felt like a form of release.

Lewis's voice was gentle, calmer. 'When I picked you up, you were running from something, weren't you?'

'What do you mean?'

'You looked scared. I can't imagine your life is easy with this—' he cleared his throat '—this ability.'

'I had a boyfriend, and we broke up. I just needed to get away, you know, forget him.' Tess stopped. She could tell Lewis about seeing, but not about Benny, not that.

'Ah,' he said. 'I don't think it ever gets any easier with love. I used to think it might, but I guess I haven't had much luck.'

'Yeah.' Let him think her heart was broken. Perhaps it was. Although she wasn't sure it was Benny who had done it to her.

'So you can see what people are thinking?' said Lewis.

She shook her head. 'No.' Benny always thought that's what she could do. He said it was why he got high. He called her a freak.

'It's hard to explain. It's more like, you know when you dream, the pictures you get in your head?'

'Yeah?'

'It's like that, but I can see other people's pictures. Not all the time, just . . .' She buried her face in her hands. 'It sounds dumb.'

'Does it embarrass you?'

'I'm a weirdo.' She kept her eyes shut so she wouldn't have to look at him, and her voice was muffled by her hands. She felt him touch one of her hands lightly, pull it away from her face.

'We're all weirdos, Tess.'

She felt shy but she looked at him. He wasn't judging her. His mind was elsewhere.

'I loved her.' His voice had a crack in it. He looked at her again and she saw who he was thinking of. 'I'm sorry,' he said. 'I'm so sorry.'

There was such discipline in the way he hid his grief, but it strained him.

'What happened to your wife?' she said.

Lewis breathed out heavily. 'Do you really want to know?'

'I do.'

He tipped his head back and looked at the ceiling. 'Nicky and I had arranged to go away, just for the day, an outing. I had a locum in, and I told Hannah that I was going to visit Mum. She was starting to decline, forget things, so I'd go visit once a week.

'Nicky and I went on a day walk, in the bush. We had to go out of town if we wanted to spend any real time together.' He paused and took a breath. 'I used to hunt, it was a way to get time by myself, the twins were full-on when they were little, and Jonti . . .

'Anyway, that morning, God knows why, he had the hunting rifle out and was cleaning it. He was always good with machines, like me. He could work out how anything operated. I don't know why but he had it on the deck.' He shrugged. 'Jean said he'd just carried it out to get the new cleaning fluid that was in the laundry. Anyway, the safety wasn't on, even though he swears he checked it because I always told him to and he wasn't stupid about that stuff. Hannah came out to tell him to get a move on for school, and the gun went off. She was shot through the head.'

Lewis touched his forehead, where Hannah was shot.

'She died instantly. Jean came out and found her brother with the gun, her mother dead on the ground, blood and brain tissue everywhere. She tried to call me first. When she couldn't get hold of me, she called Alan, who called the police and the ambulance. Then me again. No one was picking up the phone at surgery, because Nicky was with me. The cops tried to find me all day, trying my mum's place and the office, and no one could find me. My kids were alone all day without me, and their mother was dead.'

He stopped. He wasn't crying, but his face had a strange frozen look. 'I was going to leave Hannah. Things had been bad for a few years. But she was depressed, and just so angry a lot of the time with Jonti, with both the kids. God, it was such a mess. It still is.'

'It's the first time you've really mentioned him, Jonti.'

'Well,' he said slowly. 'You see, Jonti can't say a thing about it. He can't remember anything that happened that day, like his memory just disappeared. From the trauma.'

All the old hurt, the stuff she knew he kept at bay with whisky and sleeping pills, she could see it flood back into him. He made a low moaning sound, a naked sound, and then he began to weep. He let himself go in front of Tess, and she watched as everything he'd anchored so deeply in himself rose to the surface. After a few moments she placed her hand on his back, tentative but soothing all the same. He didn't move and neither did she. He continued to cry and she continued to comfort him.

After some time, Tess said, 'Would you like a cup of tea?'

'Yes, that would be good.'

Tess busied herself at the bench. She could feel Lewis watching her and she kept her back to him. She knew what he was going to ask next, she probably would too. But she hated it. She wasn't a crystal-ball gazer, a witch. That's how Benny had treated her.

'I'd like you to meet him.'

She turned to him, the teapot in her hand, and gave him a hard look. Then she turned back and busied herself at the sink.

'Why?' she said.

'I just thought you might find it—' He stopped, perhaps realising how he sounded.

When she turned back, she was trembling slightly and her cheeks were red. 'That is why I don't tell people, Lewis. It's why I can't live around them. I can't help you. I can't help your son.'

'I'm sorry. I didn't mean it that way. Or maybe I did. I don't know. You won't meet him anyway.'

'Why is that?'

'He's in an institution. He's heavily medicated and he won't see me. He sees Jean, but Jean won't see me now either. We had a fight six months ago. She stormed out and I haven't heard from her since. So—' he held his hands in the air '—that's why I live alone.'

'That's quite a shit story, Lewis,' she said.

'I know,' he said.

Tess had another picture of him in her mind, of the day they met, the determined look on his face as he pointed the air rifle at the thugs who were threatening her.

'Given what happened, you were pretty crazy to get a gun out in the main street that night.'

'The Roses are the crazy family in this town. Well, until someone else does something worse, which is possible.' Lewis laughed, but it was bitter. 'Small towns are a special kind of hell.'

Tess handed him a cup tea. 'I know. I grew up in one.'

They sat drinking their tea, gently picking at the scabs in their heads. Pain had carved itself into the lines in his forehead, around his eyes, into his eyes. Somehow he'd taken the pressure out of the air. She saw he didn't expect anything of her—of anyone, quite possibly, and that realisation made her sad. He was just like her. Neither of them thought anyone could love them. They were outcasts.

He touched the cover of the book she'd been reading. 'I read this to the twins. It was old-fashioned even then. The story was so slow.'

'I like it.' She stood up. 'I'm going to bed.'

'Yes, it's late. I should get to bed too and pretend to sleep.'

She was at the door of the kitchen when he called her name and she turned to him.

'I'm very pleased we met,' he said. 'And I'm sorry about, you know, before.'

'Kissing me?' she said.

'Yes, that.'

'It's okay. Let's pretend it never happened,' she said. It sounded harsher than she meant it to. Even though he'd been thinking of someone else, there was a gentleness in the way he'd kissed her, so different from Benny. But she couldn't say that, so she said, 'I'm pleased I met you too, Lewis.'

She walked down the hall and climbed into bed, bone tired. In the dark she listened to Lewis doing the things he did at night. The clink of the whisky bottle against the glass, five minutes later him washing the glass out, turning off the lights, moving down the hallway to his own room. She thought of his son, Jonti, killing his mother by accident.

But who was the woman in the garage? She had assumed

it was Hannah. But she hadn't seen her face, just her hair, and from that she'd made assumptions. Why did she even see her? A chill ran down her body, she could feel it lifting the hairs on her arms, bristling on her spine. There was something wrong with her brain still.

She lay in the dark for hours, restless and rolling over and over, and when she finally fell asleep she dreamed of him, a faceless boy she knew in her dream was Jonti. He was outside her window, and he was softly calling her name. *Tess,* he was calling, *Tessie.*

The next day Tess was back working in the garden when Toby started barking. She heard footsteps on the gravel driveway. A man around Lewis's age came around the back of the house and stood by the garage, looking out at her. Toby rushed over to him, and the man patted the dog's head and called him by his name.

'Hello?' Tess shaded her eyes to see him better.

'Tess, I'm Alan. I'm the doctor Lewis called when you were sick. I'm an old friend of the family.'

She walked over, taking off her gardening gloves and dusting her hands on her pants. He held out his hand to shake. Her memory of him was vague.

'You look well,' he said. 'Much better than last time I saw you.'

He had a cool gaze, and a will to contain himself. He looked from her to the garden, surveying the boundary she'd been working on, then back to her. There was possessiveness in the way he looked at the property.

'You've done all this work?' he said.

'Yep.'

'I've been on at Lewis to get the garden sorted for a while.'

Tess met his gaze, but his eyes remained glassy, unavailable.

'The garden was Hannah's, of course,' he said. 'She was a wonderful gardener.'

Something in Tess bristled, and she straightened her back a little. 'She did some interesting planting. I'm discovering all sorts of things under the growth and weeds.'

'Ah, so you're a gardener also?'

'Yes.'

He watched her, as if adjusting weights on a scale.

'Where are you from?' he said. His tone was suddenly chillier, the question pointed.

'I'm travelling,' she said. She dug her toe lightly in the gravel. 'I'll head south when the apple season comes.'

'Ah, not at uni then?'

'No.'

'My daughter is studying law. She went to school with Jean.'

Act bored, Tess told herself. 'Okay,' she said, and she could hear the hint of sarcasm in her voice but she didn't care. She just wanted him to leave. He wouldn't be played by white trash, though.

'I care a lot for the Rose family,' he said.

Bullshit, she thought.

'They've had a hard time, and I'd like to make sure things go well for Lewis.' His tone was smooth, used to being listened to.

'So would I.' Her voice was hard and she was pleased by it.

'Would you?' he said. 'So once you've got the garden in order you'll be taking off again. Picking apples?'

'I'm an arborist,' she said, lying. 'I advise on tree health, and I can pick if they need extra hands.'

'Ah,' he said. Whether he believed her or not, neither of them cared now they were locked in battle. 'I'm sure you'll be needed elsewhere then.'

Tess met his eye. The glassy surface looked darker, cold, and still gave her nothing to see. Evil, she thought. Not like Benny, but still evil because you fear and hate anything different from you. Anything you can't control you want to be miserable. 'You must have patients waiting. Doctor,' she said.

Tess turned and walked back to the garden. She could feel him behind her, mind ticking over. He was not the sort of man to allow someone like her the last word.

'I'll come again soon, Tess,' he called out. 'To check up on the tree health here.'

Tess didn't acknowledge him, but pulled the finger as she walked away. He couldn't see it but it made her feel better. She listened to his footsteps fade down the gravel path, then she started the endless task of pulling weeds.

She cut into weeds, working hard so she had a sweat. Toby sat on the deck and watched her. The sky was covered in cloud, a welcome break from the sun, but still it was hot and she couldn't clear the doctor's tone of voice, his smug face, from her mind's eye. *What a creep.* The evening swim would help. She would drown him as she swam.

As she thought of the diving in, her attention slipped and the knife she'd been using to hack at a branch nicked the side of her index finger. She yelped. Blood ran out of the wound and down her arm, but her other hand was covered in dirt. She felt faint, so looked away from the bleeding and walked as steadily as she could manage back to the laundry. She wrapped a clean rag around the cut and went through to the bathroom to find the first-aid kit. Her finger was throbbing and she felt irritated for allowing Alan to distract her. She cleaned and dressed the wound.

Tess went into Lewis's study. It was a room she'd dusted lightly, not wanting to invade his privacy. But now she walked in and went directly to his upright filing cabinet. She opened the top drawer and leafed through the files with her good hand.

School reports for Jean Rose and Jonathan Rose, tax forms for Lewis Rose Dentistry, manuals for kitchen appliances, expired passports. The letter from the hospital was at the back. Tess looked at the top of the page and started to read slowly.

Jonathan Michael Rose, admitted 15 February 1997. At the bottom the form had two signatures, Alan Williamson, MD and Lewis Rose. Alan had admitted him, and Lewis had signed the form. Tess read the address for Lakeview Institute. They always gave these places nice names, as though the residents went there for a holiday. She folded up the piece of paper and put it in the back pocket of her jeans. It was one o'clock. Lewis wouldn't be home for at least three hours. God knows what he did all day. He didn't seem to have many patients.

She changed out of her dirty clothes and went out to test the old bike that was leaning up against the side of the house. Its chain was rusting but the tyres were okay. Her finger was sore. Still, she could ride one-handed if she needed to. At the sight of the bike on the driveway, Toby started barking and running around her in circles.

'You like a ride?' she said to him. Toby eyes were wide, his whole body wagging.

She set off, the dog running at her side.

Lakeview Institute was hidden by pine trees on a hill with no lake in sight. Tess hated pines, lonely haunted trees that sucked nitrogen out of the soil. She cycled in through the large open gates. Toby had kept beside her most of the way, but now he stopped to sniff and piss against the gatepost, so she climbed off the bike and pushed. The drive darkened and the trees above her creaked and swayed. In the distance she heard the thwack of a club against a golf ball.

Where the stand of trees ended and the hill opened up she could see a long single-storeyed building, smaller than its gated entrance promised. Its brick shell was painted white and it looked like it had been dropped there without thought, on a hill out of the way. She put her bike down and held her hand up to the dog. 'Stay,' she said, and he gave a small whimper but lay down by the bike, tired. She walked up the stone steps and pushed open the door.

Inside was antiseptic, thick air. A woman was on the phone behind the front desk. She gave Tess the smallest glance and continued her conversation. Tess stood at the counter patiently. The woman turned to her with one hand held over the phone's mouthpiece.

'Visiting hours ended at one.'

'It's just . . . I don't live here. I'm passing through today and I was hoping to see my cousin?' Tess opened her eyes wide and bowed her head slightly. It was, she realised, a gesture copied from the dog.

The woman sighed. 'Hang on,' she said into the receiver. She looked Tess up and down. 'You need to phone first, love.'

The woman's breath smelt of coffee. Tess smiled and apologised. The woman sucked on her big cheeks.

'Who's your cousin, then?'

'Jonathan Rose.'

The receptionist looked at her watch. Tess thought of a fat hen sleeping on a perch.

'He's in the garden with Sal. You can go through.' She squinted at Tess. 'What side of the family are you from?'

'Oh, uh, the father's. But we haven't seen each other for a few years, not since . . . My mother was keen that I come.' *My imaginary mother who knitted me scarves in the winter.* 'Jonti and I played together when we were little. In the sandpit.'

'Go through the back. It's Sal you want.' She pointed to some doors behind the reception area.

Tess went down a long corridor with a few closed doors off the side. Through the next set of doors was a canteen, the smell of fatty mutton and boiled vegetables. Long stainless benches with empty bains maries. It was a joyless scene, but the windows looked out onto a large stretch of lawn and, beyond that, a stand of flax where a group of people were working along rows of dirt, hoeing and weeding.

Tess pushed through some doors that led onto a wide wooden porch and walked towards where the people were working. As she got closer, the gardeners looked up. They were all male. Tess thought of cattle, raising their heads from grazing. She smiled, to show she meant no harm. 'Sal?' she called.

'Here!' One of the men looked up and waved his arm at her.

'I'm here to see Jonti Rose,' Tess said. The workers were spread out over a large area of fenced vegetable garden. 'This is an impressive patch.'

'Yep, we're aiming to get half our food from it over summer. Ambitious eh!' He focused on her now, intent. 'You family?'

Tess held his gaze to let him know she was safe. 'Kind of. I'm a second cousin. I don't live here, just passing through.'

Sal nodded to beyond the vegetable garden. 'He's good today. He's trimming the edges.'

'Eh?'

'Over there.' Sal pointed to where a young man with a crop of wheaten hair was bent over at the border of a patch of long grass. His posture was awkward, stiff. Tess couldn't figure out what he was doing. 'Follow me.'

As they approached, the young man bent further over his work as if blocking them from seeing it. But they got closer and Tess could see now: he was holding a pair of kitchen scissors, trimming the grass to make a rising line along the tops. He was precise and attentive with his method, and did not acknowledge them even when she and Sal were right beside him.

'Jonti.' Sal's voice was soft. 'You have a visitor.'

The young man didn't stop his trimming, nor did he look around.

Sal held his hand in the air in a patient gesture at Tess. 'What're you making today?' he said.

Jonti was silent for a few long seconds, then gave a rough grunt. 'Camel.' His voice was deep and flat.

'Awesome!' Sal smiled at Tess. 'Jonti is our in-house artist. We keep this grass long for him and he cuts it into creatures, just with those scissors. But you can only see the shape from above, like on a ladder. The local paper did a story on him when he cut the horse. What else was there, Jonti? A horse, a dog—'

'Toby,' said Jonti.

'Toby?' said Tess.

Jonti glanced at her. His blue eyes were like Lewis's, but clouded, closed to her, as if hidden behind the thick metal door of a safe. His eyes were half-lidded when he spoke. 'Toby is my dog.'

'Yes, I know Toby,' she said.

'Toby is in the grass,' said Jonti. 'I made him in the grass.'

'Yeah, it was awesome,' said Sal.

Jonti stood there, his hands by his side, as if waiting for them to leave.

'This is your cousin, Tess,' said Sal. 'You remember her?'

Jonti shook his head. 'No,' he said. 'No, no, no. No cousin, no cousin.'

Sal looked at Tess, apologetic. 'I'm not sure if—'

A dog barked, and Tess and Sal turned. Toby was bounding over to them. Jonti made a humming sound and his face broke into a grin. He knelt down, and the dog ran up to lick him.

'Toby?' said Sal.

Tess nodded. On the ground, Jonti's posture loosened. The dog nuzzled into his armpit.

'I've heard about Toby, but I wasn't sure if he was, you know, still around. It's cool you brought him in. Are you staying with—?' Sal gestured at Jonti.

'Yep.'

'I wish we could keep animals here, it would help these guys, I reckon.' He looked over at the garden. 'Aw, shit. Sam! Put the dirt down! Take it out of your mouth!' He turned to Tess. 'Hang on a minute? There's only one of me.'

'It's okay.'

Jonti was rubbing the dog's ear between his thumb and index finger. Toby was peaceful, his head on Jonti's leg. Tess knelt down, keeping space between them. It was clear he didn't like anyone too close.

'Toby likes you a lot.'

Jonti lowered his head, scratched at his neck. His cuticles were rimmed with dirt, his fingernails cut short. The nail on his left index finger had a black ridge through it. *You're going to lose that one*, she thought.

'You're not my cousin,' he said.

'No.' She looked back at Sal. 'I'm staying with Lewis. He . . . he wanted me to bring Toby to see you.'

'Toby is my dog.'

'Yes.'

'Toby is a good dog.'

'He is,' said Tess. She smiled.

'Toby is a good, good dog.' He still had his head lowered. 'You are a liar.'

Tess felt her cheeks warm. 'I . . .'

'Good boy, Toby.' He kept patting the dog, looking down, never at Tess.

'I'm not your cousin,' she said. 'I'm sorry I lied. I just wanted to meet you.'

'And Lewis is a liar.'

'What?' said Tess.

Jonti rubbed the dog's ear between his fingers. Sal was coming back towards them.

'Why is Lewis a liar?' Tess ran her hand over the grass. 'Jonti?'

'Toby is a good dog.'

Sal was beside them. 'Sorry about that. You all okay?' He gave a nervous glance back at the garden. 'We need more staff but they keep cutting our budget.'

Jonti looked up at Sal. 'She is—'

Tess stood up quickly to interrupt him. 'I'm gonna go now.' She gave Sal a big smile.

'Oh, you can stick around if you want,' said Sal.

'I need to get back.' She gave an apologetic shrug. 'Jean could bring Toby next time.'

'Jean is mean,' said Jonti. 'Jean is mean, Jean is mean, Jean is mean.' He sang the rhyme like a child might, teasing.

'Oh, Jonti, you love Jean.' Sal shook his head. 'He's actually great with Jean. She hasn't been for a while though.' He screwed his face up. 'Have you seen her?'

'I think she's in Wellington.' Tess sounded vague. She needed to get out before Jonti said anything else and she was found out. She should be back in Lewis's garden, or back on the road, not tangling herself up in other people's problems. She had enough of her own.

'Jonti, you can work on your camel again,' said Sal. 'Here are your scissors.'

Jonti stood and turned back to the long grass. Tess didn't know if his compliance was his own or his medication.

In the middle of Jonti's grass the bleached seeding tops were softly dancing. Jonti reached out, as if to touch them and run his hands over their outline. He turned to her and saw she was looking at him. If there was anything for Tess to see in him, it was so small, so delicate, she couldn't bear to see it, even for a moment, and she looked down at the dog waiting patiently by his side. *I know*, she wanted to say. *I know what it feels like to be locked inside your own head.*

Then she saw he was looking at her boots, the ones she'd found in Jean's closet and put on because her sneakers were wrecked from walking. They were short leather boots, with elastic sides, quality ones that were old and worn but they'd started to soften as she worked in them. She liked them. She wanted to keep them.

'They are Jean's boots.'

'She lent them to me.'

'Jean's gone away.'

He looked at her, and she suddenly could hear birds in him, a flock rising. Screeching birds, birds skittering in your head, claws on glass, birds being chased by birds of prey. He lived with that noise.

He patted the dog's head and the noise dimmed.

'Good Toby,' he said. Then he turned back and continued to cut out his grass camel.

Tess walked the bike home with Toby loping beside her, his tongue out. The heavy cloud had moved out to the ranges and the sun burnt fierce through a clear patch of sky. The air was thick and she felt winded by it all. She hadn't imagined how Jonti would be, but it made sense now she'd met him. In some respects, he wasn't so different from her. She just hid her strangeness better. People like Jonti, like Tess, weren't cut to fit this world.

Just as they reached the driveway, Toby sniffed, picked up his pace and ran off across the front lawn and around to the back garden. Tess wheeled the bike up the gravel and leaned it against the side of the house, thinking of the last bit of work she'd do before Lewis got home. She was tired, deflated, but she could do another hour at a slow pace. She came around the corner and saw what Toby had run to.

On the back lawn, in the full glare of the sun, a young woman was lying on a towel, wearing only her bikini pants, her breasts bare. A thick pelt of yellow hair spilled around her head like a wild halo. It was startling: something was both natural and staged about the scene—like glossy pictures in a *National Geographic* of a lioness grooming herself. The woman was beautiful.

Tess knew who she was from the photos Lewis kept on the mantelpiece: Jean. And there was Toby, already lying on his back, submissive beside her, as if he'd been there all afternoon. Her hand was on his stomach, and Tess could hear her talking to him low and soft. Tess wanted to call out, to indicate she was here, but her voice was stuck in her throat.

Tess thought of the lioness, but also of a queen, a queen of some superior tribe. Jean's body indicated possession of her domain, luxuriant on a towel, as if the towel were an extension of the house and the garden, and both were in her sphere of control. Her skin was tanned and her breasts were like those in the *Penthouse* magazines Benny kept under the bed. Tess had not seen breasts like this in real life. She'd paged through the magazines when he was out, running her hand over those glossy bodies. There was something thrilling about these women with their breasts like perfect cakes. Her own were insignificant lumps on her chest, barely flesh. How reduced she felt next to women like this, a weed grown in the shade, whereas the young woman in front of her was a hothouse plant. Tess cleared her throat. Jean startled and sat bolt upright.

'Who the fuck are you?' A look of annoyance on her face. But she didn't cover her breasts, just glared at Tess.

'Sorry, I didn't mean to frighten you.' Her voice sounded pathetic, apologetic. 'I'm Tess. You're, um, Jean, aren't you?'

'Is that your shit in my room?'

Jean's sunglasses slipped down her nose, and Tess caught a quick glimpse of her blue eyes before she pushed the glasses up again and placed the large hat that was beside her on her head. She looked like her twin, like Jonti, but the model version of him, still undamaged through the short course of their lives. She had, Tess saw now, the flawlessness of a private school girl. More than that; she was the template for that girl. They were a separate category of girl, untouchable, unfathomable. She used to stare at them whenever she saw them in town, with their expensive sports satchels and their straight, tidy ponytails that flicked when they turned to comment to one another, hands held over their mouths. They had special rules about what was proper, like not eating on the main street while in school uniform. Their skins were flawless, never pimpled. Even if they were freckled they had the right kind of freckles in neat bands across their noses. Smooth skin, the right sunglasses and sun hat, bikini bottoms, the right breasts and tan, hems always at the right length. As these girls became women they would continue to wear perfection like an aura; they would marry the right men and their children would be the right children.

Looking at Jean, Tess suddenly knew she'd been wrong about Lewis—about who he was, about who his children were. This knowledge came on her like a chill and she wanted to leave, to go now. She'd met the broken version of Lewis, but she should have guessed from the nice things in the living room, from the books on the bookshelves. She should have seen that they came from different sides.

'Lewis gave me your room to use. I was sick—'

'That sounds like Lewis.' Jean raised her nose in the air as if she might smell an answer to what she asked next. 'What are you doing here?'

'I'm helping in the garden. Lewis gave me a lift. I was sick.'

'You already said that.'

Jean gave a bored sigh and lay down, cutting off the interview. Her hat toppled behind her and she didn't reach for it, but left it as if there would always be more hats, or more people pick up the fallen hats for her.

Tess stood frozen, wanting to get away but unable to.

'Quit staring,' said Jean from behind her sunglasses.

Tess rocked on her feet before she could make them move.

'Your stuff's in the hall,' Jean called out behind her. 'And I want my boots back.'

Tess walked through the kitchen, hearing her heart thumping in her ears. In the hall, Jean had thrown everything everywhere. Tess's jeans, underpants, hairbrush, T-shirts, her holed shoes, even the book she'd been reading were strewn up and down the hall. Tess took off Jean's old boots and put them neatly outside her closed bedroom door, then she sank to her knees and began to gather her things and stuff them in her pack. It only took her a minute to put her life's belongings back inside, and when it was done she stared at the faded canvas. It had been Benny's pack. He'd had it when they met and she liked it: it looked like something to go out into the world with, although he'd only made it as far as a month with his aunt in Brisbane. They had talked about going overseas with the money they got from Doug. Then Tess had taken the pack, so now it was hers, but she hadn't gone so far either.

Tess took a breath to steady herself. She would make herself a sandwich and write a note to Lewis. Then she would leave.

Everyone's got something they want to keep hidden, Benny would say. *The difference with you, Tess, is you can see it.* She tried to explain to him that it wasn't that simple, that she could only see what people vividly remembered, and if someone really wanted to hide something, they would. There were people who could bury things so deep inside it was as if they'd forgotten altogether.

Doug lived in the same block, a few flats down from Tess and Benny. Tess had seen him coming home from work, going off in the morning. He didn't say hello or smile the way some of the other tenants did. He was grey in his manner and his way of dressing. He wore a cheap suit, the jacket always crumpled at the back. He seemed to avoid looking at anyone. Tess imagined a life for him—a job in an office in one of those grey-walled cubicles in which people pin comics about people working in offices. Doug would sit behind a computer. She had no idea what he might do on the computer, only that his imagined office gave her a desolate feeling. If he'd met her eye she might have seen something, but he didn't and she liked to wonder—there was freedom in that.

Benny ignored their neighbours. He called them lowlifes, as if he and Tess were above them, as if they didn't live among these people.

One of her habits was to sit on a stool outside their door and drink her coffee and watch the kids play below. She observed the hierarchy established, the jostling for places. There was one big girl, Anita, who was developing early, her breasts already pushing bumps under her T-shirt. She ruled the roost. New kids would move into the building and would need to go through a set of exercises and questions set by Anita. Tess watched it silently. It was a miserable scene where children played out their dramas. One of swings was broken; the see-saw moaned when it was used. There were no trees. The children were animals in a too-small pen.

Tess had arranged a few pot plants outside their flat door when they first moved in, some rosemary that she thought would be hardy. But it got torn out the first week, and when she got another it went brown in a month and made everything look worse. Benny teased her and called her black-fingers. *Where do you think we're living? In some fucking country garden?* But it wasn't her, it was the air and the motorway behind the block. The whole place was toxic. How could anyone grow anything there?

Tess had stopped to rest before climbing the stairs. She'd walked home from the supermarket because she'd run out of money for the bus, and her shopping was heavy and she put it down to search her jacket pocket for her keys. Her fingers ached where the bags had cut in as she carried them. When she looked up, she saw Doug looking down from the door to his flat. He hadn't seen Tess. He was watching with complete concentration a young girl, new to the block and not yet one of Anita's acolytes, swinging alone in the playground. Tess saw what it was and felt sick. It was shrouded in shame and it was a rotten thing, but there it was, a part of him. Instinctively she moved out of the shade into the sun so he would see her. She lost sight of Doug's face with the sun in her eyes, but he saw her and she made sure she looked at the girl and then back at him, so he knew.

*

It was a few days later that Tess mentioned Doug to Benny. She didn't tell Benny much anymore. It seemed to Tess that her own feelings had shrunk down to a tiny kernel inside of her. To hide herself like that felt bad, but at least her most private self was untouched by Benny.

'I got an idea,' said Benny. 'You can do your thing on him. A guy like that, I bet he's got secrets, worse than just looking at some kid in a playground. Go and knock on his door and look him in the eye, see what he's got.'

'Why?'

'Fuck, Tess, sometimes you're slow. If he likes fiddling with kids we can get money out of him. I owe Matt a grand now. I've got to get money to him somehow.'

'You said you'd stopped dealing.'

'And I have, baby. It's an old debt. Matt's calling it in.'

He moved closer and put his arm around her. 'Come on, Tessie. You gotta help me out here. I'm the one earning all the money for us. And guys like that need to be stopped. The cops won't do a fucking thing until he does something real bad and someone complains, and what would you have been doing? You could stop him, and earn some money doing it. We can ask for 5k, pay Matt and bugger off overseas with the rest.'

He looked so pleased with his idea, so certain, whereas everything in Tess screamed no. She couldn't reckon with this gap between what they thought sometimes. She couldn't understand where Benny's head was at.

'I could just put a note under the kid's door? Address it to her mother?' she said.

'Yeah, but what's the mother gonna do then? She's gonna

knock on his door and accuse him and he'll just move on to some other kid. You gotta squeeze guys like this where it hurts them most.'

He kissed her and stroked her hair. When he was trying to get something out of her, Benny was at his most gentle. He'd call her Tessie and his voice would be so soft. *Tessie, baby.*

The clouds had turned back from the hills to spread dark and low over the town; the wind was getting up. Tess held her thumb out with only two goals—to get away as quickly as possible, and to keep dry—but the traffic passed her without slowing. Farmers' wives going home with children and shopping, trucks moving the evening paper, the milk. Then she saw the Zephyr. It slowed, pulled over and stopped. Lewis opened the door and stood, one foot on the road. He was peering at her, the same expression on his face as the first time he'd stopped for her.

'Get in,' he said. 'You can't just leave like that. The radio's predicting thunderstorms.'

He looked past her to the heavy sky, and she saw how tired he was, worn out from their conversation the night before, from the return of his daughter.

'Lewis.' She was determined. 'You've got other stuff to deal with.'

A stream of cars passed. Lewis watched them, impatient. 'Where the hell are you going anyway?'

'I don't know,' she said. 'South, I guess.'

He didn't speak. She looked at him, and his face drew pity out of her. He was more lost than she was.

She walked over to the car and got in but didn't close the door. They sat there silent for a time.

Finally he said, 'So, you met Jean.'

'Yes.'

'I love my daughter, but I'm aware what a bitch she can be.

Like—' He stopped. 'Actually, like her mother. It's hard to live with. Fucking impossible sometimes.'

'It's okay,' said Tess.

'No, it's not,' said Lewis. 'It's me she's angry at. She doesn't need to take it out on you.'

A few light spits of rain hit the windscreen.

'Hey,' he said, 'the garden will like this.'

'I guess so.' She was stubborn, not willing to give way.

'You could just stay until New Year? It's Christmas next week, you know.'

Tess thought of Sheila, wheezing alone in that horrible room. It was stupid how people made so much fuss out of Christmas. 'So what?'

'Yeah. I'm as excited as you are.' He paused. 'Jean says she's going to bring Jonti home for Christmas lunch.'

'Does Jonti want to come?'

He shrugged. His face was cloudy, confused. 'We've always done what Jean tells us. It's kind of irrelevant what we want.'

'I dunno, it might be good.' Tess thought of Jonti down on the ground, patting Toby.

'It might be. But as you can see, I'm not asking you to stay for entirely unselfish purposes.'

She shook her head. 'I don't want to be in the middle of your fights. You can't use me.'

'I don't want to use you! It's just, another person around, it might . . . There's no one else I can ask, Tess.'

The rain was more persistent and the road ahead looked bleak. It wasn't as if she had so many choices. And here was Lewis, pleading with her. There was something she liked about it. It soothed an ache in her, like Sheila sitting beside her on her bed, rubbing her forehead because she'd been calling for her mother in her sleep. She nodded at him and closed the car door.

'Thank you, Tess. I mean it.'

'I know you do, Lewis.'

He started the car and turned it back towards town. And now the rain came hard like many hands beating down on the roof, a thin shell between them and the onslaught.

That night they ate their dinner with the loud battering of rain on the roof. Thunder in the distance, angry shadows approaching. Tess said a silent thank you for not being out in it.

Jean had looked up from her position at the table when Tess walked back in with Lewis. She pulled her lips in tight and opened her eyes wide at Tess, but she said not a word and didn't speak all through the meal, except to ask Lewis for twenty dollars. He reached over to his wallet on the sideboard, took out a note and put it on the table at the head of his daughter's plate. The simple movement of a hand reaching across a table to give, the giving when asked. Tess wondered if this was what most fathers and daughters were like. She had no comparison. She looked at the money sitting on the table and she wanted to reach out and take it, put it in her own pocket. It was that easy for Jean to get money. Jean didn't say a word, didn't even pick the money up, just looked at it and put her head down at her plate again to finish her meal.

And even when the room pulsed with brilliant blue light and the thunder cracked loud, and Lewis and Tess looked out the window to spot the bright line in the sky, Jean pretended that none of this was happening, as if she wasn't in the room with them. When she finished eating, she reached for the money and pocketed it, took her plate to the kitchen bench and left. Lewis looked at Tess. He shrugged and exhaled, as if to say, *What am I supposed to do?* Tess didn't say, *Not that. Not that useless thing.*

*

After she'd done the dishes, Tess walked out onto the deck. The rain hadn't let up and with the light from inside the kitchen she could see it, straight like arrows to the ground. She wanted to witness the earth soaking it up, the large roots of the trees and the tiny roots of the new seedlings opening their mouths and drinking. But the flowers on the beans and tomatoes were still delicate; they would bruise in such hard rain. A shiver ran through her, a delicious chill that came from being comforted by the safe confines of the house. She knew that if Lewis hadn't come after her she'd be out in this.

A voice spoke from the dark, and Tess startled.

'What do you think you'll get out of him?'

She hadn't seen Jean sitting on the hanging chair in the dark corner of the deck.

'What?' said Tess, though she knew exactly what Jean meant.

Jean didn't speak, but Tess could hear her all the same, demanding an answer.

'I don't want anything,' she said finally.

'Right.'

There was a rustling in the dark. Tess saw Jean stroke the long white roll of the cigarette, smoothing it in her fingers, then hold it to her mouth and flick her lighter. Her eyes squinted as she sucked on the end; the flame faded and Jean breathed out.

'So how many blow-jobs will it take to pay him back?'

Tess balled her hand at her side. It always shocked her when a person didn't disguise their hate. She could feel a tremble start up in her body and she willed it still. She would not let Jean frighten her away again.

'You don't have a clue what you're talking about,' said Tess. She turned around to go back inside.

'Don't walk away from me!' It was an order and a plea,

confusion in Jean's tone.

'You want me to stand here so you can abuse me?' said Tess.

Jean growled in her throat. 'That's better. You're so fucking passive. No wonder Lewis likes you. But you know what? I think you're a disgrace to women. You'll just take whatever a man will hand you.'

Tess felt a storm in her that threatened to pick her up and throw her down if she didn't take control. This girl in front of her was doing that to her. Tearing at her, pulling on her in a way she'd never felt before. Tess looked out at the dark wet garden. If she could call the lightning down right now, upon Jean in her chair, she would. She ran her thumb over the welt on her index finger. It throbbed beneath her touch.

Tess spoke in slow hard syllables. 'You. Don't. Know. Any. Thing.'

'I don't need to know anything. It's all there for me to see.'

'You can't see a thing, Jean.'

The strength of her own tone surprised her. Jean might be her superior in many ways, but not in every way, and Tess knew that out of the two of them she was the one with the sight, not Jean. Yet she also knew Jean was toying with her, prodding her until she forced a crack. It was something she'd probably been doing forever, pushing people until she broke them, like a cat toys with a mouse, stressing it, tiring it, taking delight in the cruelty of the hunt. Tess admired Jean's raw intuition, her guesswork. Jean's eyes were hidden in the dark, so Tess was denied her natural advantage, and she wondered briefly if Jean knew what she could do, if Lewis had said something. But Tess trusted him not to give her away, not even to his daughter. If Jean knew to sit in the dark, it was her good instincts, not knowledge.

'Why have you come back?' said Tess.

Jean lit another cigarette and Tess saw the red tip flare in the dark, and—briefly—Jean's eyes. The hanging woman was in them.

'I got fired. Not that it's any of your business.'

Tess knew she was telling the truth, but Jean was smart and good-looking enough to pick up another job easily, especially around Christmas. It couldn't be the whole truth. If she hated Lewis so much, losing a job wasn't enough to bring her back.

'I hope you didn't blow him on my bed,' said Jean.

'What?'

'Lewis. I hope you didn't suck Lewis's cock on my bed.'

There was loathing in Jean's voice, but it wasn't for Tess; it was just fired at her because she was here. Jean was lost. Tess could see that now. She was floundering around in the dark with a knife, not knowing what she was stabbing at, just needing to stab. Tess knew then that the woman in the garage was Jean. She'd come home to kill herself.

She rocked back on her heels a little and looked straight at Jean. 'What makes you think I'd want a man?' she said.

The two women stared at each other. Jean's face was genuine surprise, and Tess tried to stay strong, steady in her own gaze, and then she remembered Jean on the grass, her hair spread, her bare breasts, and her cheeks went hot and she broke the gaze, looking down.

Then Tess heard Lewis behind her. How long had he been standing inside the doorway?

'You're at your most hospitable, I see, Jean.' Lewis's voice was tense.

'Fuck off, Lewis,' said Jean.

He paused, steadied himself in the doorway. 'You're many

things, Jeanie. But kindness was never your strength.'

'Ha!' Jean spat back at him. 'What would you know about kindness, Lewis?'

'I'm your father,' he said. 'Please show me some respect.'

'You are so full of shit.' She sucked on her cigarette. 'Has he told you, Tess? Has he told you what he did to my brother after our mother died?'

Tess stood still. She didn't want them to play their troubles out for her, she didn't want them. What she wanted was to disappear. At that moment she wanted to be what Jean accused her of being: an invisible woman.

'Jean!'

'Uh-uh, Lewis. You want to make Tess feel right at home? No secrets, Dad. That's what you always used to tell me and Jonti. No secrets. No lies.'

Tess could feel Lewis shaking beside her.

Jean sat back in her chair, defiant.

'I'll tell you the story, Tess, seeing as Lewis won't. After my mother's brains got blown out all over our deck, Lewis, this same kind Lewis who's been so selfless in helping you, instead of helping his own son, who he knew would fall apart in an institution, he had him committed to a fucking psych ward and pumped full of drugs till his mind was so fried he couldn't remember a fucking thing. His brain was munted. His beautiful brain . . .' Jean's voice was wobbly. She threw her cigarette on the deck and mashed it down with her foot. 'How's that for kindness, Lewis? How's that for respect?'

Lewis was angry now. 'Jean!'

'What, Papa? You don't want our house guest knowing our secrets? Why not make her right at home? She should know what she's getting herself into.'

Lewis shook his head. 'Not like this.'

'Then like what, Lewis? You haven't even been to see your own son. You've broken him completely. That's not kindness, Lewis. That's as fucking cruel as you can get.'

'He can't be here, Jean. I only make him worse!'

She muttered, 'No fucking wonder.'

They were silent then. Through the rain they heard an engine, a raw muffler, wheels on the wet gravel. It stopped and idled around the corner of the house. A horn tooted once.

Jean stood up and put her shoes on.

'Where are you going now?' said Lewis. 'That's not Cody, is it?'

'That's not Cody, is it?' Jean parroted.

'I know what he is.'

'What, Lewis?'

'Don't be coy, Jean. He's a dealer. I'm not stupid. He threatened Tess in town. He's dangerous. I don't want you going round with him.'

'People stopped going round in the eighties, Lewis. Catch up. We're almost in the year 2000.' Jean rolled her eyes. 'And you know what? Go inside and look in the mirror. Then open up the bathroom cabinet and see how many fucking drugs you've dealt for yourself.'

She walked off the deck into the rain. 'Good fucking night, y'all.'

Lewis and Tess watched her go into the weather. There was a blast of music as she opened the car door, then a door slamming and a car revving as it backed fast down the driveway. Then it was just the sound of the rain on the deck, water splashing down in a narrow fountain off a hole in the guttering. Tess turned to look at Lewis, whose face was bowed away from the light, but she could see he was breathing fast, as if gulping at the air, like someone having a heart attack. He made a noise, and she imagined his chest prolapsing, his lungs leaning against his ribcage. Tess reached her arms out, and he bent over and wept into her shoulder. She stood there holding him. After a few minutes, he quietened down, lifted his head and rubbed his hands over his face.

'I'm sorry,' he said. 'It's Jean, she really knows how to push me. I want to see Jonti, I really do. He just gets so upset when I go.'

Tess knew Jean wanted to break her father, but she also knew she'd seen a chink in Jean. When she'd said that Tess couldn't see what was in front of her, Jean was describing herself. It was Jean who was waving her arms about, unable to find a way through.

'When the kids were three, Hannah left us. She walked out. She'd had depression, though it wasn't diagnosed. She'd never get help for it. I think she probably had some sort of breakdown. Twins are hard and Jonti never slept, and then as he got older we knew he was different but no one could say what it was. Anyway, Hannah came back after two months, and there was something of a fracture between us, between her and the kids, especially between her and Jean. It was . . .' He shook his head. 'And Jonti needed extra help anyway. He was always different, always difficult. He never had friends, no one other than Jean. Then, later, Jean found out about Nicky, because Hannah told her. Hannah used to do that sort of thing, play the kids off against me. It was wrong of me to have an affair, but it was wrong of her to tell them. She shouldn't have done that. Anyway, Jean thinks I hated Hannah. She thinks I wanted Hannah to die.'

'And did you?'

'God, no. Not like that. I didn't want to be with her, but dying . . . It's such a mess. I'm sorry, I feel bad asking you back. I guess I thought—I don't know what I thought.' He shook his head. 'She's right, too. I did write myself scripts after Jonathan was committed. Codeine, diazepam, anything I thought would help. I just wanted to stop feeling for a while. Alan found out and made me quit. I was very close to losing my practising licence.'

'Have you stopped?' said Tess.

'Pretty much. Mainly alcohol now. It's legal.'

They sat on the deck watching the rain and lightning play out. A word popped into Tess's head, one she'd heard but never used in conversation because she didn't know what it meant.

'Lewis,' she said, 'what is a maelstrom?' She didn't know if she was saying it right. But he obviously understood, because he laughed.

'Jean,' he said. 'Jean is a maelstrom.'

Sometime in the night Tess woke to a door slamming. She heard Jean in hallway, brushing her teeth, going for a pee. On her way back down the hall she stopped, just outside Tess's room. She was quiet, but Tess could hear her, breathing on the other side of the door. Tess held herself very still, and took shallow breaths, willing Jean to move away. After a minute she heard Jean's bedroom door close. She breathed out, and tried to calm herself, but she lay there restless, not falling asleep again until the early morning. And when she did sleep she dreamed that Jean, her chest bare again, was standing over her, one hand on Tess's throat, while in her other she gripped Benny's knife.

Over the next few days, there was a wire held tight between Tess and Jean. They didn't speak much, but Tess could feel it, pushing and pulling her around. Tess worked in the garden and Jean lay in the sun, sometimes clothed and sometimes with just the skimpiest knickers on. Every now and then Tess would turn to look at her. She felt she could feel her, watching. But when she turned Jean would have her eyes closed. Tess never managed to catch her looking.

Toby had abandoned her side for Jean. She missed the dog, but understood his loyalty, admired him for it.

Jean spent most of her nights out, returning late. Lewis told Tess he worried about her.

'Is she being civil to you?' he asked.

'Yeah, I guess,' said Tess. Mainly Jean seemed to ignore her and Tess decided that she wasn't going to be the one to try to be friendly first. It wasn't up to her.

'Well, tell me if it's a problem, I mean, if she's rude.'

'Sure,' said Tess.

Lewis seemed to think that was enough.

Tess was lying on the bed in Jonti's room, reading. It was too hot outside and Jean was always there, sunbathing and smoking. She heard Jean moving around in the kitchen, down the hall. Then Jean was standing in the doorway, looking at her.

'You read a lot,' said Jean.

Tess looked up.

'When you're not gardening.'

'Hm,' Tess said.

'Another kids' book?'

'Yup.'

Her eyes were back on the page now, not reading but pleading silently for Jean to move away. Jean stood, tapping a rhythm out on the door frame.

'Do you ever, like, have fun? Go crazy? Dance?'

She made cross eyes at Tess, and Tess found herself grinning. She didn't know what to say, though. She looked back at her book.

'Suit yourself,' Jean said, and moved away down the hall, back to the kitchen.

Tess stared at the space where Jean had been, trying to figure out what she had wanted, what was going on between them. Whatever it was, it was making her tired, the heat and this moving around another person, acting as though she wasn't there when in fact she was hyper-alert to Jean's every movement in the house and garden. Tess let her eyes close, and soon she was asleep.

When she woke it was almost five o'clock. She went through to the kitchen for a glass of water. She wouldn't work anymore today. She felt sleep-heavy, overheated.

Standing at the sink, filling her glass, she could smell it. Sweet and bitter and always accompanied by a strange taste, as if she held fine metal filings on her tongue. She walked out to the deck. Jean was in her chair, lighting a small pipe.

'Oops,' she said, breathing out a cloud of smoke. 'Caught me. Don't tell Lewis.'

'I wouldn't.' There was a hint of annoyance in her voice, which she didn't mean.

'You want some? Is that what you're saying?'

Tess shook her head.

Jean held her free hand in the air. 'No dope for super-girl?'

Tess looked at her hard. Had Lewis said something? Jean was holding the lighter up to her pipe and sucking on the end again.

'What?' said Jean. She coughed.

'Why did you call me that?'

'What, super-girl? Cause you're doing all this shit for my father. Just out of the goodness of your heart. And look at it—the garden looks like a garden again, but different to how it was. It looks . . . nice.'

Tess listened for the sarcasm, but it didn't seem to be there.

Jean held out the pipe. 'Sure?'

Tess shook her head.

Jean shrugged. 'It's good, it'll take your mind off things.'

'I don't have things to take my mind off.'

'Lucky you.'

She heard Jean as she walked away. 'Liar, liar, pants on fire.'

That night, just as they were finishing dinner, Jean went into the sideboard, grabbed a box and threw it down on the table.

'Scrabble. Let's play,' she said. 'Like a real family.'

'I . . .' Tess screwed up her face. 'I've never played.'

'Good. I'll cane you.'

'Jean!'

'I'll cane you too, Lewis.'

'A fun time then.'

‘I think I’ll just watch,’ said Tess.

Jean stared at her, critical. Tess thought of always being chosen last for sides. People complaining when she was the only person left and they had to take her. Always dropping the ball, not because she couldn’t catch a ball, but because they expected her to drop it, and so she did, even if she’d caught it, she’d drop it again.

Lewis and Jean played. Tess hugged her teacup and watched. The game involved long periods of quiet while they moved around some blocks with letters on them, then Jean would growl and tell Lewis to hurry up. Letters that made no sense propped up on a wooden stand. Jean’s said: K W E B V R T. When Tess leaned over to look at them, Jean, without turning around, said, *Quit it!* and Lewis said, *Jean.* Jean complained because Lewis had taken all the vowels. And Lewis said, *You can’t win a game with vowels*, and, *I didn’t choose to take them.* Jean told him to shut up. But Lewis did not shut up. He stood and poured a very large whisky, while his daughter wore her scowl. Lewis smiled and said, *The wind might change, Jean.* Tess wondered if they were actually enjoying themselves. Lewis knocked the first drink back, poured another. *That’s right, drink yourself to a loss, Lewis.* Lewis dark. *You know, it’s so much fun playing games with you, Jean.* Tess didn’t say a word until Jean turned to her and said, *Aren’t you pleased you stayed, Tess?* And Tess, refusing to look at either of them, said, *Good night.*

Brushing her teeth in the bathroom she heard the tiles scattering over the floor. *Jean! Stop acting like a child!* Stomp. *I was just trying to liven things up, but you’re all so fucking boring. She won’t play, and you just get drunk.* Silence. *You know, Jean, when other people get stoned, they chill out.* Stomp, stomp. *Fuck you, Lewis.* Slam. Lewis shouting after her, *I'm not picking up the fucking tiles.*

Tess pulled the covers up over her head, tried to block out any further noise. It was like they couldn't not do this to each other. Girls at school would complain about their parents not letting them do this or buy that, and Tess would smile, like she understood. Those few times when Rose had come to see her at Sheila's she'd been so spaced out. *I'm trying,* she heard her tell Sheila when Tess was out of the room. *Can I borrow a hundred bucks?* The last time she'd come, Sheila had tossed her out. *If you really loved your daughter you'd clean your act up,* she'd said. *It's your fault*, Rose had shouted at her. Tess blocked that out now. She hated to think of Rose—the strung-out shell she'd been reduced to. She wished Toby would come into her room—the dog never argued—but he'd stayed in Jean's room since she'd come back.

Sleep came slowly and it was a wild weather she dreamed she was out in, rain and thunder, and she couldn't find her way home. She woke with a start and sat upright. *Where's home? Where's home?* The question was clawing at her, climbing in her throat. She put her hand on her chest to calm herself. Inhale, exhale. The room was light, the night calm, full moon. The plants and insects would be going crazy. The thought of all that growth made her feel tired, and she lay back down.

The sound from the other room was at first barely perceptible, then soft, then a keening made quietly but at a pitch she couldn't ignore. Tess got out of bed and stood in the centre of her room, listening to make sure she wasn't hearing things. Then, certain she wasn't, she walked through to Jean's door, pushed it ajar and moved just inside. The light was off but Tess could see the long form of her, lying on top of the bedclothes, her back turned away from the door.

'Jean.' Tess's voice was soft. 'Jean?'

The dog was sitting beside the bed, his big head resting on the mattress, eyes on Jean's back. He looked briefly round at Tess, then back to his mistress.

The keening went quiet but Tess could see her body shaking, trying to contain whatever it was that wracked her.

'Piss off,' said Jean.

'No.' Tess's eyes were adjusting to the dark of the room. Clothes and shoes were flung all over the floor, and there was a stale smell of cigarettes and underneath that a rotten smell, like meat going bad. 'What's wrong?'

'I said piss off!'

Tess stood there, uncertain what to do next. Then Jean spoke again.

'Don't come near me. I'm disgusting.'

Her voice was low and, Tess thought, for the first time true.

Tess walked over to her, knelt down and put a hand on the curve of Jean's spine. Her back was sticky with heat. Jean didn't roll away or speak, so Tess kept her hand there, thinking how she didn't expect someone so physically perfect as Jean to be so sticky.

'No, you're not,' said Tess.

Jean turned suddenly and sat up, her face right up close to Tess's so that Tess got the heat of her breath, the stale dope smell of her.

'I am.' Her voice was fierce, willing Tess to agree.

'I don't think so. I think . . . that you're beautiful.' These words surprised Tess, not the thought itself, but that she was saying it out loud.

Then Jean's lips were on hers, soft, but pressing like she meant it, her tongue reaching into Tess's mouth, and all of Tess's breath went out of her, and a voice inside her said, *Yes. Yes, of course.* Her own cheeks dampened with Jean's tears, and Tess wiped her hands over Jean's face to clear them.

Jean's lips just above Tess's own and Jean whispering, 'Did you know? I wanted this?' Kissing her throat so Tess could feel the movement of her voice box against Jean's lips.

'No. You were horrible to me.'

Jean spoke low but fierce into her mouth. Her eyes peered into Tess's, demanding truth. 'I thought you were doing Lewis.'

'Well, I wasn't. I wouldn't . . .'

Jean's lips on hers again and hands through her hair, roughing it and pulling it at the roots, desperate. In the dark of the room their bodies were feeling out the newness of each other. Tess wanted the proximity of Jean's body, her breasts against Tess's own flat chest, the softness of her. She didn't think. All that seemed to be required was for her to respond to this woman who wanted her. And, Tess realised, she wanted her back. She hadn't known it, but this was what she'd wanted from the first time she saw her lying on the grass like a barely domesticated cat.

Jean pressed on the shard of Tess's ring, and cried out, *Oww, that fucking ring of yours! You're so tiny and you wear a dagger on your finger.* Tess said, *Sorry*, not wanting to explain, but not wanting to hurt her either. *Don't apologise*, said Jean. *I love it.*

How long their touching went on Tess could not say. But there was a moment when Jean pulled her down so they lay beside each other and rolled one on top of the other. Tess felt alert to everything—to the night air, to the heat of Jean's body against her own, their hands reaching for each other's buttons and zips and pulling on their clothing, on any restraints that bound them from each other, and Tess marvelling at how soft Jean was beneath the spiked carapace she displayed to most people. She could have guessed how sensual she was just from seeing her lying on the towel that day, nearly naked, but she would not have guessed at this softness that yielded to her and was somehow a complement to Tess's bony angles. Jean covered them, delighted in them, where Tess had only ever seen herself as a skinny, insubstantial girl, and now Jean was calling her *Lovely, you're so lovely*, and Jean's fingers were stroking the line down her waist, the jut of her hip bone around to her buttocks and between her legs and Tess was moaning, and believing her, believing Jean that she was lovely, thinking too that Jean made her so.

And why, she wondered, when this first urgency had been spent and it became a delight to simply lie against each other, skins stuck with sweat and Jean's cigarette making a red hole in the dark air of the bedroom; why had it taken her so long to know this was possible in the world? That this was what she wanted?

In the morning Tess woke to Jean's fingernails on her back.

'I'm writing you a message,' said Jean.

'Uh,' said Tess. 'Don't.'

'It's a nice message.'

'It's just . . . I don't read very easily.'

'What do you mean? You're always reading!'

'I read kids' books, and it takes so long just to read one chapter.'

'How come?'

'The letters don't stay still.'

Jean rolled onto her elbow. 'Are you dyslexic?'

'I don't know. Maybe'

Jean's eyes were wide. 'What school did you go to!'

Tess looked down at the sheet and smoothed it out with her hand. 'I didn't go much.'

Jean ran her finger in circles at the small of Tess's back. 'Jonti's dyslexic. The words move around for him too. But he can read. He taught himself. I mean, he reads science texts and animal psychology books now. He's very focused, when he decides to do something.'

Tess watched her. Jean's face softened when she talked of her brother.

'Do you miss him?'

Jean scowled. 'Of course I miss him.'

'Hey,' said Tess.

Jean exhaled, looked back. Jonti was there, but he was being led away, two men at his side. Then her face cleared.

‘Concentrate,’ said Jean. ‘I’ll do one letter at a time.’

She ran the tip of her index finger on the middle of Tess’s back.

‘K,’ said Tess. ‘I. S.’ She rolled on her side and kissed her. Soft mouth, the sense of being bound to this woman in her arms.

Jean pulled away with a start. ‘Do I look fat to you?’ she said.

How could Jean even think this when she was so perfect? ‘You’re beautiful, Jean,’ Tess said.

‘You didn’t answer my question.’

‘Well . . .’ Tess looked at her directly. ‘This is what I feel. Next to you I feel like I’m all skin and bone and nothing. Whereas you’re like a woman from a painting, all soft and . . . what’s the word they use?’

‘Please don’t say fleshy.’ Jean screwed her nose up.

‘Why not? It’s a good word.’

Jean rolled on her back and sighed. ‘My mother was always on a diet. She’d watch us eat at dinner, and she’d pick away at some lettuce or a few peas, wearing this look on her face, like she was missing out and hating that she was missing out and hating herself for hating missing out. I only just realised this year that was how she felt, because I went on a diet, and I was out with some friends and they ate pizza and I pretended I wasn’t hungry. And I hated them and I thought I was better than them because I was hungry. I used to feel guilty eating with Mum at the table, like if I ate a lot I was a pig.’

Tess touched her cheek. ‘You don’t need to diet. You’re perfect.’

Jean shook her head. ‘No. Don’t even say that. I come from a totally fucked family, and you said it last night, I’m a bitch.’

Tess protested but Jean covered her mouth gently with her hand.

'Just listen to me,' said Jean. 'After she died, part of me was happy she was gone, because I could just eat and not feel bad about it. But then I felt like I was evil for thinking that, and it was as if she was sitting there anyway, watching us. And Lewis's meals were pretty shit when he first started cooking. Chops that were all bloody and vegetables cooked to mush.' She shrugged. 'I stopped eating meat because of the way he cooked it. And I started throwing up. You know . . .' Jean put her fingers in her mouth and pretended to gag.

Tess leaned over her. 'You're not evil. You are beautiful, beautiful,' she whispered, then kissed her. 'Though sometimes you are a bitch.'

Later, she said, 'What shall we tell Lewis?'

'Why do we have to tell Lewis anything?'

'You don't think he'll notice I'm in your room?'

Jean shrugged, 'Who cares?'

Her eyes offered Tess nothing but what she had now: Tess reflected in Jean's eyes, and Jean in Tess's. 'How many girls have you been with?' said Jean.

'Well . . .' Tess was shy. 'Just you. This sounds silly, but until last night I hadn't thought too much about it—I mean, not actively. I always liked them. I had a weird upbringing, not many people around me.' She paused, but somehow it was easy to ask Jean these questions. 'How many have you been with?'

'You really want to know?'

Tess nodded.

'I've been told I'm a slut.' The way she said it made Tess

laugh. It wasn't a word to be ashamed of when Jean said it. 'You've been with guys, though? Like me?'

'Yeah.' Tess tried to look casual. It was too soon to explain Benny. 'But nothing serious. I don't think I've ever been in love.'

'Me neither. I don't even know what it would feel like. How would you know?'

They lay on their backs watching the morning sun move a bright line across the ceiling. Outside, birds were busy in the ash tree.

'But I've never felt like this before.'

'Like what?'

'Happy.'

Tess did not know if she was waking or dreaming. The days were gardening, swimming at the river, kissing Jean, her jaw aching from kissing and smiling—she couldn't stop smiling. Nights spent fucking. She remembered someone at school saying that it was only boys who could fuck. But Jean called it fucking and that's what it was, and it had never been like this with Benny, not this playful, serious, funny, strange fucking thing. Some nights Tess found herself crying, not from sadness, but from something that overwhelmed her, joy so acute it was almost pain. She was revealing herself. *You've undone me,* she said one night. *That's how it feels.* And Tess wanted to be undone, remade. In the garden, Tess showed Jean the purple flowers on the beans, the yellow ones on the tomatoes, flowers where fruit would grow. Jean said she didn't know why it was called fruit when beans were vegetables. Tess said it was the process, the process of fruiting. Jean turned the hose on her. Days spread out like a soft down on which she'd been invited to roll around. When had time ever been so luxurious? When had air and breathing?

The closest thing to this timeless feeling of days was the hours she'd spent in the garden with Sheila, who'd sit on her garden chair beside her, talking. Sheila telling her stories about what she'd seen in her life.

'Once I saw a dog grieving for his owner who had died. I could see the owner in the dog's eyes, throwing a ball. Dogs are very loyal, you know.'

Tess said she didn't believe her about the dog, but Sheila said it was true and that Tess could think what she liked, it didn't change the truth.

'What about cats?' said Tess. 'What about Tama? Can you see his memories?' Tess didn't like Sheila's cat Tama, mainly because he didn't like her. Tama was old now, ancient and grumpy. He lived in the cave of the old hot-water cupboard, even though it wasn't hot. He ate and shat there, and when anyone other than Sheila opened the door he would hiss and bare his claws.

'Don't be stupid!'

'Doesn't Tama have memories?'

'Yes, but cats don't open up to us, they keep everything very private. Did I tell you about old Kamala, though? The elephant at the Wellington Zoo?'

Whether she made them up or not, Tess liked these stories of Sheila's, the glint that came into Sheila's eyes when she told them.

'Now Rosie, your mother. She was a one! I saw her first kiss. A sweet boy, Mike Christian. Not that bright, but Rosie had liked him since they were in New Entrants together. He used to share his jam sandwich with her. Well, she was fifteen and she came home from school one day, later than usual, trying to hold in this big grin. And I could see it, like a movie projected before me, those two kissing, hiding out in the flax bushes. I didn't say nothing. But I smiled. I shouldn't have bloody smiled. I had no right to. After that she wouldn't look at me, not properly. She hated the seeing. I can't blame her, because she couldn't see.'

'Could she really see nothing?'

'Zilch. Blind as a bat! It was what made her leave home, get involved with that crowd.' Sheila shaking her head. 'She told me she wanted to be around normal people. Well, look how well that worked out.'

Tess didn't know what to say. She often wished she had a mother, but not Rose as she was. Her life had been better since she'd lived with Sheila.

'I know you think she didn't love you, but she did. She just couldn't be a good mum, and she knew it, not while she was so messed up. There was always something missing in Rose and it made her weak. I think she got it from her father's side. You know the other thing? I think Rose bringing you here was her telling me that I could help you. That you and I could help each other.'

Tess didn't say there was nowhere else her mother could have taken her.

'I never told you before, but I saw a murder once. Not the real murder itself, but I saw it in this man's eyes. He'd killed his brother's wife. He was a teller in the bank, so I guess he'd got away with it. He was in love with her, I could see that, and I could also see he couldn't have her. So he killed her. I used to do all I could to avoid him when I went in. And he was a judgemental bastard. I'd see his nose pinch up and his eyes go all squinty when he had to deal with me, you know, a woman on a benefit. So one day I gave him a look. And when he handed me my money, I said, *People do terrible things in the name of love, in the name of what they can't have.* And I walked out.

'And what did he do?'

'He said, *What?* in his dopey voice, like he hadn't heard me, but he'd heard me. His eyes went dark, and I could see he was scared. Next time I went in, he was gone. Never saw him again. It's true, Tess. People do terrible things for what they call love. But there is a love that opens your life up in wider and wider circles. It's the opposite of destroying each other, of wanting that turns you crazy.'

Tess looked at Sheila but she couldn't read her. Sheila could do that, she could keep a part of herself locked away, out of reach of Tess.

'Before you were here I was going mouldy, like old bread. And then Rose brought you here, Tessie. She brought you to me.'

That night, after they'd had sex, and Tess was falling asleep, she thought of Sheila's eyes and she felt she understood now, and without thinking, as if her mouth were connected to her heart, not her brain, she said, 'I think I'm half in love with you, Jean.'

Jean's body went rigid beside her, yanking Tess out of her slumber.

'What?' said Tess. She knew what she'd said, but perhaps it was wrong, perhaps she'd been dreaming, sleep-talking. In the silence, Tess could hear Jean breathing, could feel her making an answer. A way out.

'I'm impossible to love,' said Jean.

Tess thought of the image of her, Jean hanged in the garage, and she wanted to shout, *No no no no!* That had to be a nightmare, so she held Jean tight, so tight her muscles trembled with the effort.

'No one is,' said Tess.

But she wondered as she said it, what about Sheila's bank teller, who killed his brother's wife? Was he possible to love? Had the woman he killed loved him too, even though he killed her? Had she, Tess, loved Benny? She hadn't felt like this around him. Not this *possible.*

'I feel like my whole self is safe with you,' said Tess.

'Really? Even when I'm a bitch?'

'Yes,' said Tess, 'even then.'

Jean rolled onto her back and Tess could see her eyes shining in the dark. Large, alert, animal. She wanted to tell Jean, to tell her about seeing, and she even opened her mouth to begin, but there was no sound available to her. There were so many things to say to Jean, it was hard to know where to begin.

'I went to see your brother. You know, the day I came home and you were practically naked on the lawn? I'd been to see Jonti at Lakeview.'

Jean was silent a moment. Then, flatly, 'Why?'

Be careful, Tess told herself. 'I don't know. It seemed important to find out who he was.'

'Important to you?'

'Yes. And just . . . Lewis seems so miserable.'

'He deserves to be.'

'Why?'

Jean shook her head. 'Because he fucked up. Anyway, I don't want to talk about Lewis.'

'Alan came here that morning,' Tess said. 'He came when I was sick, and it was like he'd come back to check on me. Because he wanted me gone.'

'That's Alan. He acts like my mother is still alive. Part of her head was missing and her pulse had been gone for twenty minutes and still he pumped away at her heart.' Jean's voice was a monotone. 'He's supposed to be a doctor.'

'Shit.' Then it hit her. 'He was in love with her?'

Jean nodded, slow, because it was only just obvious to her too.

'That's why he acted like he owned this place,' said Tess.

Jean turned to Tess then, eyes wide. 'I didn't know it, but now I feel like I did know it all along. Ew, gross. I wonder if they ever, you know . . .' She shook her head hard. 'I don't even want to think about it. He's so . . . ergh, old and straight. What did she see in him?'

'Do you think she liked him too?'

'I dunno—' Jean cut herself off. 'How can I know? What's the point in wondering?'

There was no point in wondering, but Tess had done it for years, even though it was painful to wonder about things that were impossible, like having a mother. Tess used to imagine what her mother would look like now—older, but still with her long, slightly proud neck, her shy smile. *Rose grew into her looks,* said Sheila. *She was one of the lucky ones. Such a pity, such a waste.* Tess was fifteen when Sheila said this, and she had been hurt by it because she thought Sheila was saying that her mother had intentionally wasted her tiny fortune, her face. But now Tess got it. Sheila had imagined a life with Rose still in it, and this wasted her, just as it wasted Tess, but neither of them knew how to stop longing for it. Squandered, desolate love.

'My mother was a junkie.' Tess shivered to say out it out loud. 'She OD'd when I was sixteen, but I hadn't seen her for years by then.' Sheila and Tess had never talked about it because they couldn't. Sheila had seen it, and perhaps she guessed that Tess had, but she was too caught up in her own grief and rage at the stupid waste her daughter had made of her life. 'She took me to live with my grandmother when I was five because she couldn't look after me.'

Something went through Tess then—a gale ripping through bastard pines. Knock them down, she thought, rip those fucking trees out at the root. And it burst out of her and she wept and Jean held her; Jean held her tight, and kissed her on the tips of her ears and whispered that she was here, *I am here*, and everything would be okay, *everything will be all right.*

Tess took half the money. It was fair, and Benny might not come after her, at least not so quickly, if he had money as well. She grabbed his pack and stuffed what she could into it. Then she wrote a note. *Keep away from the man in Flat 11.* She slid it under the door where the girl lived, and walked away from what had been her life.

Later, she thought how stupid she'd been to leave that note, to leave evidence. She had time to think such things, walking.

Once she was out of the city she kept to the old roads, off the highway. She didn't care how long it took, where she slept or where she got what she needed. It was funny being in a stranger's house when they weren't there during the day. The people who didn't lock their houses were her favourites, not because they were easy to get into, but because of the trust they displayed. And Tess respected it and took only what she needed. Fruit from fruit bowls, bread from the pantry. Fizzy drink stored in the fridge door. Once an old man came home when she was at his table, drinking a cup of his tea. *Hello, Goldilocks*, he said. His eyes were a tiny bit afraid. She stood up at his table, *Thank you*, she said and then she ran, like the girl in the story. Strangers could be kind. But then, they didn't know what she'd done.

Her first thought had been to stop Benny, just stop him. *Mind the artery*, she'd shouted, and still he'd gone in again, and the blood on Doug's leg was bad, there was too much of it outside his body and his face was so pale. So she swiped the ring that

Benny had bought her through his eyeball. She cut Benny's nose, and his cheek. The ring had been a gift from him. *It's for defence, you know. If anyone ever comes round to the house when I'm not here.* Tess had said, *What do you mean? Who will come here, Benny?* It was later she learned about his debt to Matt, that he'd been skimming the top off the cash from his deals. *Can't be a middleman all your life.*

Benny spoke so confidently, like he was in charge, but Tess had met Matt and she knew the pecking order. When he'd dropped stuff off for Benny, he'd stood in their small galley kitchen, drinking a glass of juice that he'd helped himself to from their fridge, leaned back against the bench with his legs wide.

That time at the pub when he'd looked at her like he wanted to bite her, like she was something to be eaten and discarded. Benny went to the loo, and Matt pressed the length of his thigh against her and said, *Do you get lonely when Ben's working?* He looked at her when he said it, but all she could see in his eyes was himself. His teeth were bad and his cheeks stuck to his cheekbones. Her first thought was that he would look bad as he got older. She pulled her head away from him and narrowed her gaze. *What made you like this, Matt?* she said. He pulled his thigh back, as if it had been touching something gross. *Fuck, you're weird.* And chugged the rest of his pint.

Benny had tried to punch back at her, but his eyes were shut with the shock, and then the pain, and he cupped his hand round the wound, so she couldn't see what she'd done. *What the fuck, Tess! You cunt, what have you done!* And immediately she wanted to cup her own hand around his eye and tend to it.

Sheila's voice in her head was saying, *People do terrible things in the name of love*, and Tess was momentarily confused, because she was supposed to love Benny the way he swore he loved her and couldn't be without her. Benny's blood was flowing through his cupped fingers and she'd done that to him and she knew then that to stay and help him now would be a terrible thing. So she ran. She ran to their flat, packed her few belongings, split the money and called an ambulance. Then she left.

For two weeks after she would listen out for news: alerts to the public about a young female witness. But there was nothing. If the cops or Benny were looking for her, they were doing it quietly.

So,' said Lewis at dinner, 'it's nice to see you two getting along finally.'

Tess smiled at him and Jean kicked her leg lightly. Neither of them had told Lewis yet, and Jean had said that morning in bed, *I wonder what it would take for him to notice. I mean, would he have to walk in on me licking your pussy for him to get it?*

'Yep, we are, Dad. Tess and I are getting on very well.'

Lewis looked thoughtful. 'I'm pleased for you. I'm pleased for you both.' He smiled at them knowingly, and continued to eat.

'Dad?' said Jean.

'Yes, dear?'

'You know?'

'Know what, Jean?'

'That I'm a muff diver.'

Tess coughed on her mouthful of food. Lewis put his fork down and scratched his head lightly. 'That's not quite how I'd put it, but yes, I did know.' He smiled. 'Jean, all I've ever wanted is for my children to be happy. That's been very hard to achieve, much harder than I thought. But in the last week I've seen you happier than you've been since you were a little girl. I see the effect that Tess has had on you, on our household, and I'm very grateful.'

'Oh.' Jean's face had gone pink. 'Okay.'

'Are you happy, Tess?' said Lewis.

Tess looked at him, kind Lewis with his sad eyes. She nodded.

'Good,' he said.

They ate in silence for a few moments. Then Jean, mouth full of food said, 'Hey Dad, any other lezzos in our family?'

Tess was splayed back in Jean's arms on the deck while Jean smoothed her hair and told her stories of the kids she'd been at school with.

'Emma Hinton, who used to give blow-jobs for twenty dollars in the cleaner's cupboard behind the hall stage. She always got top marks in class and the teachers liked her so she never got found out. But everyone called her a slut.'

'Why'd she do it?'

'Money for jam? Maybe she liked it.' Jean shrugged. 'James Kennedy, he died last year. He was like this rugby dude that everyone liked, fell asleep drunk with a cigarette and burned to death. Vanessa Peat was pregnant with his baby at the time. She had an abortion. Now she's going out with Wiremu Johnson.'

'What about your friend, the doctor's daughter?'

Jean breathed in sharply. 'Lizzie?'

Tess looked back at her. Jean's face reddened, and Tess could see Lizzie, her back turned.

'We don't really talk anymore.' Jean's hand had stopped stroking Tess's hair. 'I thought I was in love with her. She knew too. She told me I was disgusting. That what I wanted was disgusting and unnatural and that I'd been using her. So we're not really friends anymore.'

'When did this happen?'

'In Wellington. Just before I came back.'

Tess sat up. She held Jean's hand in hers. 'That's why you

were so sad when you came back, eh.' She thought of Jean, hanging in the garage.

'Yes. But then I met you.'

'Yeah.' Tess moved her head into Jean's until their noses touched. 'And that feels like the best thing in the world.'

They heard the engine gun out on the street, then the sound of wheels in the driveway.

Jean pulled back. 'Fuck.'

'Is it that guy?'

'Cody? Yep. I think he has a thing for me.' Her face was grim.

Tess watched the car pulled up outside the garage. Cody got out and raised his eyebrows. 'What up?'

'Not much.'

'Haven't heard from you in a week. I wondered if you were still here?'

Jean shrugged. 'I'm still here.'

'Who's that?' He nodded at Tess like he'd never seen her before.

'My girlfriend.'

'Your wha—?'

'My girlfriend.'

'Really?' Cody screwed his face up, disbelieving.

Jean reached over and kissed Tess on the lips. 'Yep.'

'Shit, Jean,' said Cody.

Tess, brave beside Jean's own toughness, said, 'I've met you before.'

He scrutinised her face. 'Nup.'

'You tried to grab me on the street.'

'What?' said Jean.

Cody's eyes had gone blank, impossible to read. He ignored Tess. 'Jean, you owe me a hundy.'

'Yeah, I know, I'll get it to you.'

'I want it now.'

'I said I'd pay. I'm good for it. What did you do to my girlfriend?'

Cody shrugged. 'I don't know what that bitch is talking about.' He turned, calling out as he walked away, 'I know where you live, Jean.'

On Christmas Day, Jean went to collect Jonti in the Zephyr. *Don't crash my car!* Lewis shouted as she walked out.

Tess was wearing a pinny and beating egg whites when they returned. Jean said, 'Look, Jonti, this is Tess. Doesn't she look cute in an apron?'

Jonti stood in the doorway, head down. 'Tess is a liar,' he said.

'Hm,' said Jean. 'But not all the time.' She placed her arm lightly on her brother's back.

Standing side by side, Tess could see the twin-ness of them, and realised that Jonti was teasing her the way his sister did him. *Tess is a liar.* Did he know about her and Jean? Or did he somehow know what she could do? Was this his way of questioning her?

Then Lewis came through, and halfway across the kitchen stopped and stared at his grown children, astonished. Tess watched him. She was learning his face the way she was learning the local weather patterns. She wondered why she'd ever thought his face was closed. He was the opposite of that, she could see it now—he was too open, too vulnerable. This was what Jean turned away from in him.

'Jonti,' he said. 'Happy Christmas, boyo.' He rocked off his heels and walked over to the sideboard, picked up a brown paper bag. 'Sorry it's not wrapped.' He held out the bag.

Jonti didn't move, kept his eyes on the ground. Jean was looking at him, and Tess saw she was nervous. This had been her idea, that Jonti come home for lunch. Toby stood beside him, looking up, tail moving lightly. The dog could read the tension, but he was a dog, a natural optimist. Jonti made a stiff reach forwards and took the gift from Lewis. He held it with both hands, nimbly tracing the edges of the gift with his fingertips, his eyes half shut.

'I've read this one,' he said.

'Just open it, Jonti,' said Jean. 'That's what you do here. You open it and even if you've read it ten times, you look surprised and say thank you, what a nice present.'

'I've read it seventeen and a half times.'

'What was the half?'

'Sal spilt his coffee on page 141 and I couldn't finish it because it was ruined.'

Jean laughed. 'Well,' she said. 'It's good Dad got you another copy then.'

'Hm,' said Jonti. He unwrapped the gift and nodded. 'This is the right edition. It's got the revised introduction and they corrected the typo on page 23.'

Jean poked Jonti on the rib. 'Thank you, Lewis,' she said, imploring.

'Yes,' said Jonti.

'You're welcome, son,' said Lewis.

Lewis, Jean and Jonti went through to the living room. Tess stayed in the kitchen and finished the pavlova mixture. She'd never made one before. She was following the Edmonds recipe, which Lewis said was a never fail, and Jean said, *How do you know? You're a pavlova virgin, Lewis.*

Tess beat the sugar in, slowly like the recipe said, and the white transformed from something brittle into unctuous gloop.

She stuck her finger in and it felt like satin. The mixture, when she tasted it, left a lingering stickiness in her mouth.

She could hear them talking in the living room. Not what they were saying, but she didn't need to know that to hear the tone in their voices when Lewis and Jean spoke to Jonti: tentative, yes, but happy. Then Jean called her through.

Jean was holding out a gift to her.

'I thought we said we wouldn't buy presents for each other,' said Tess. She hated how wary she sounded.

'I didn't listen to you,' said Jean.

'But I didn't get you anything.'

'I've got what I want, Tess.'

Tess's face flushed. Jonti was studying the two of them from the sofa. When Tess caught his eye, he lifted his book and pretended to keep reading.

Tess felt the package in her hands, a box wrapped in gold paper with a red ribbon. Sheila and Tess would give each other one present at Christmas, something they'd made themselves. They never had money for buying stuff.

'Open it,' said Jean.

Inside was a shoebox. Tess took the lid off—a pair of silvery-white plastic sandals. The sort of shoes you might wear to a party.

'Jellies!' said Jean, and when she saw Tess's confusion she laughed at her. 'You never had jellies? When you were a girl? I didn't think so. They're the best shoes. They give you blisters, but they look choice. Try them on.'

Tess slipped the shoes on her bare feet. Jean leaned over and did up the silver buckles for her. 'Perfect,' said Jean. Then, tentative, 'Do you like them?'

Tess looked down and tapped her sparkly feet around. 'Yes,'

she said. And then she felt she would cry. 'I'll just go check the oven,' she said, and ran out of the room. The last pair of fancy shoes she'd had were the ones she'd worn to Sheila's when Rose left her there.

Lewis set the table for lunch using the fine silver. He folded linen napkins and placed them beside the crystal wine glasses he said were given to his mother when she married his father. *She never used them, in case they got broken*, he said, and shook his head. *That makes me want to smash one now*, said Jean. Tess admired the table, and they sat down to eat. Ham, lettuce and beans from the garden, a nut-roast Jean bought for Jonti because he never ate animals now. Jean said, *You just eat food that looks like animal shit, eh?* The boiled potatoes came from Anne's garden because Tess's wouldn't be ready until late summer.

'Did Anne give you these or did you ask for them?' said Jean.

'Can't remember,' said Lewis.

Jean rolled her eyes. 'She gave them to you, didn't she. She likes you. Anne liiiikes you, Lewis.'

Lewis topped up everyone's glasses and ignored her.

'Who would win, Jean? A polar bear or a grizzly?' said Jonti.

'Grizzly, definitely,' said Jean.

He made the off-key buzzer noise. 'Wrong.'

'I'm generally not.'

'You are. You're wrong in this instance because neither would win,' said Jonti. 'A grizzly is very aggressive and can fight, but a polar bear is bigger. They'd come to an impasse and walk away from each other.'

'Trick question, Jonti. Not fair.'

'It is no trick, Jean. It's bare facts.'

He made a rough sound, and Tess saw he was giggling. It was an awkward noise, but he had a beautiful smile like his sister. She knew he'd made a joke only because Lewis and Jean were laughing.

'What's so funny?' said Tess.

Jean raised her eyes at her. 'Bare facts. B E A R facts?'

'Ohhh,' said Tess. 'I get it.'

'Do you?' said Jean. 'Do you really?'

Tess shook her head. 'No, not really.'

'It's a play on words. Tess is dyslexic, Jonti,' said Jean. 'But she reads heaps, like you.'

Jonti looked in Tess's direction, shy, with his eyes over her left shoulder. 'How do you pin the birds down?' he said.

Tess paused. She knew what he meant. 'I don't,' she said. 'I can't. But sometimes they settle on the page. I've been reading the books in your room.'

'That's not my room,' said Jonti.

'It was, that's what she means.' Jean stabbed her ham so her fork scratched her plate. 'And one day you could come home if you wanted, or get your own place.'

Tess watched Jean's face. It had already hardened.

Lewis cleared his throat. 'So, have you all made resolutions for the new year?'

'I think I'm going to study for my School Cert English,' said Tess. 'And science.'

'What?' said Jean.

'I never passed. I got maths by 53 per cent, but not English or science. Then I left. I'd like to get more qualifications.'

'That's good, Tess,' said Lewis. 'Jeanie, you could take a leaf out of Tess's book and go to university.'

'Plurgh!' said Jean.

'You'd make a great lawyer,' said Lewis.

'Dreams are free, Dad.'

Jonti cleared his throat. He sat very still, his eyes flickering left and right, up and down, thinking of a way to say what he meant to say. 'Sal has helped me enrol in a veterinary science degree. I can send the answers through email without going to the class.' He looked back down to his plate.

'Wow, that's super-cool. You never said,' said Jean.

'You didn't ask me,' said Jonti.

Lewis was looking at him and rolling his wine glass back and forward in his hands. 'Were you going to tell me?' he said.

Jonti made a grunting noise and shrugged.

'I can help pay for it,' said Lewis.

Jonti pressed his lips together tightly.

'I'm not angry, Jonti. I'm happy for you. You'll make a great vet. I have no doubt about it. I'd love for you to be a vet.'

Jonti was silent.

'Can you just tell me how much it costs?' said Lewis.

'Sal's helped me apply for a student loan.'

'It's just, your mother and I . . . we saved money for you and Jean to go to university.'

'I don't want it,' said Jonti.

Tess could hear Lewis breathing hard. Jonti continued to eat his meal.

'Give it to me then,' said Jean, and took a large sip of wine.

Then she started rocking slightly, like she was laughing, even though nothing was funny. Her face was going red and her cheeks were ballooning with air and wine in them, and then her mouth burst open and the wine she'd been holding in sprayed out over the table, over the food and everyone's plates.

Jonti scowled.

'Sorry,' said Jean.

Lewis watched her. 'No you're not,' he said.

'You're right, Lewis, I'm not sorry at all,' said Jean.

Somehow, the rest of the meal was peaceful. Jonti told them facts about animals. *Did you know that if you lift a kangaroo's tail off the ground it can't hop?* And *female kangaroos have three vaginas?* Jean snorted. *Lucky them.* Tess served the pavlova which had sunk in the middle and looked nothing like the picture in the book, but everyone told her it was delicious. Jonti ate three helpings and when he was finished he looked at Jean and said, *Take me home now, Jean.*

Tess stood on the deck next to Lewis. 'Bye,' she said. 'It was nice to hang out with you today, Jonti.'

Jean elbowed him, and he looked down at Tess's feet. 'I like your shoes.'

Tess wriggled her toes around. 'Thanks.'

They watched Jean back the Zephyr out of the driveway at speed, tooting as she went. They heard the car drive off the gravel over the bump of the drive onto the lawn, reversing into a turn, then stalling. *There goes the grass*, said Lewis. They heard Jean swearing loudly in the still air, and then starting the car again, and then they were gone, Jean gunning it away down the road. Lewis shook his head. His face was happy and sad.

Longing, thought Tess. *What are we supposed to do with it all?*

The week between Christmas and New Year's was slow. They ate leftovers and raspberries that Tess and Jean picked at a nearby orchard. They lay in the sun and when it got too hot they drove down to the river. Anne came over one day and they all went there for a picnic. That night, Lewis said she was lonely. *So are you*, Jean told him. And Lewis said, resigned, *I know it.*

The surgery was closed until early January. He would start drinking beer at lunch, whisky by three in the afternoon. Tess mentioned it to Jean, and Jean said, *Lewis, you're acting like an alcoholic.* But Lewis shrugged and said, *I'm on holiday.* Sometimes when Jean had her arm around Tess, Tess would catch him watching them. It was then she could see that woman Nicky, and Hannah. They were tangled around him like vine. Then Lewis would smile, and she could see he was trying hard to forget, but the vine wound tight.

Lewis spent New Year's Eve day on his back under the front of the Zephyr. *I'm going to fix that fucking clutch good and proper*, he said. *This car is not going to stall in the new millennium.*

Tess went out to the garage to get a garden fork; the weeds were going nuts. Lewis was mostly hidden under the car.

She spoke to his feet and ankles. 'That looks really uncomfortable, Lewis.'

'Yep,' he said.

She stood there, listening to him grunting and cursing when he clanged a spanner on the concrete.

She got down on her knees and peered under the car.

'Tess,' he said.

'Yes.'

'Don't run away from my daughter.' He was fierce under the car, demanding.

'I . . .' she began.

'I know you've been running from something. I don't need to know what. But if you need to go, take Jean with you.'

'Lewis, I don't—'

'No,' he said, his tone stern. 'I really don't want to know what happened. But I want you to understand this—I haven't seen Jean this happy since she was small. You make her happy, Tess.'

'Okay, yes.' Tess wanted to say more, to say that Jean made her happy too. She stood there a moment, willing herself to say more, but she couldn't make the words form in her mouth. 'Thank you,' she finally said. Then she turned back to the garden.

*

At five o'clock Lewis walked through to where Tess and Jean were lying on the sofa in the living room, reading and talking. Grease on his face and bare arms, black ground into the grains of his fingers.

'I'm done,' he said. 'I do believe I fixed that bloody car.' He held up a bottle, triumphant. 'I've had this away for ten years. We're going to open it tonight.'

'What is it?' said Jean.

'Moët, 1989.'

'Oooo, Lewis! Sharing your sweet stuff.'

'Only the best for you, my daughter.'

They washed and dressed for midnight. Jean put her short shorts on, because Tess said her legs looked so good in them. Tess put on her new jellies and pretended to tap dance for Jean, who laughed so hard she said, *Stop, or I'll piss my pants.* Then Jean said she was going to get a surprise and took the Zephyr out. She came back half an hour later with Jonti.

Tess watched the smile erupt on Lewis's face.

'Jonti wanted to be with us tonight,' Jean said. 'And Sal said it was cool. He has to be back by ten is all. Bit lame, but better than nothing, eh?'

'Jean made me come,' said Jonti.

'But you said you wanted to come,' said Jean.

'Because you want me to,' said Jonti.

*

Anne arrived at seven, and Jean and Tess exchanged glances. Lewis pulled the Moët out of the freezer.

'Do you think it will have lost its fizz?' said Anne.

'Yes,' said Jonti.

Lewis grinned and loosed the cork out with his thumb. It flew up and hit the ceiling.

'Nup.'

Tess and Jean sat drinking on the sofa, voices low, heads bent together. Jonti sat at the end, reading a textbook. Every now and then Jean would ask him a question about it and he'd say she wouldn't understand. Jean had put Prince on.

'The future is here,' she said, as the needle touched the record. 'I thought it would be cooler than this.'

'The future is never here,' said Jonti.

'Cooler than what?' said Tess.

'Than spending the last hours of the twentieth century with my father.'

On the other sofa, Anne and Lewis were talking about patients. Tess thought he looked relaxed, like he was actually enjoying himself.

At one point Jean leaned in and sang Prince in Tess's ear.

Jean raised her glass. 'Happy New Year, you all.'

'And to my children.' Lewis raised his glass in return. 'I love you both, very much.'

Jean lifted her head in a backwards nod, staunch, but Tess saw through it. She could see now when Jean was protecting herself. There was a crack in her, and Tess saw the crack and she recognised it because she had one herself.

There lived the mothers—Mummy, mother, Mum, Rose, Hannah. Red hot blue black mothers like the gas that sprays off the sun, like lava flowing down a new island to the sea, mothers who cool and harden to rock, mothers like hard rain bruising new fruit.

Jean stood and turned Prince up and then she came and pulled on Tess's hands so Tess was standing too, and then she pulled on Jonti's, but he refused and kept his eyes down on his textbook. Tess and Jean danced. Lewis and Anne danced, and Jean rolled her eyes at Lewis. *You're such a naff dancer, Daddy.* None of them heard the car, or the back door open and close, or the footsteps across the kitchen and up the hall, the heavy footsteps of men who feel they've been wronged. They thought Toby was barking at them, at them dancing, then Tess looked at Jonti who was staring straight past her, a strange look on his face, which made Tess look harder, and then made her turn so she saw them in the doorway—Cody and, behind him, Benny. Cody held the air rifle, the one Lewis had pointed at him in the main street.

Sheila in her head, saying, *Chickens, Tess. They always come home to roost.* And a tremor came from deep within her, plates shifting and stretching, strike-slip fault rent open.

'Huh,' she said to Jean, because her words were gone. 'Uhh.' All she had was quiet terrified breath. Jean must have felt her shiver and cool, and she turned too and saw them, and never lost her words.

'What are you doing here, Cody?' Jean doing her best to control her voice, but Tess could hear the alarm in it.

'Hey Tess,' said Benny from behind Cody's shoulder.

Lewis wobbled to his feet but his voice was firm. 'Get out of my house,' he said. 'No one invited you.'

'Whoa, man,' said Cody. 'That's not friendly. You need to calm your shit down.' Cody shook the rifle at Lewis. 'No waving guns!'

Cody and Benny laughed.

'Get out of my house!' said Lewis. There was a slight slur in his voice. He swallowed hard at the sight of his own rifle turned on him.

Benny stepped forward into the light. 'Sorry,' he said. 'We can't do that.'

'Jean,' said Jonti. 'He has a gun inside the house. Don't bring guns inside the house.' Cody and Benny laughed.

'I know, Jonti,' said Jean.

Tess saw Benny's face now, the full bloom of the cut across the bridge of his nose, scabbed up but certain to scar. His left eyelid like Sheila's pink satin pincushion unpinned, raw meat. With effort he lifted the lid to show her. The eye was dead. She'd gouged it dead.

'How did you find me, Benny?' she said.

He looked back at her with his right eye, his one good eye.

'You know I got the contacts. I know people, Tessie.' He shook his head. 'It was unreal when Cody said his girlfriend had gone for this chick who'd come from nowhere. And when I asked what her name was and he said, Tess, I just knew, I just had this feeling in my gut . . .'

There was a tremble in his voice. He could barely hold himself in. She kept looking at the eye she'd blinded.

'You can't see anything there now, can you, Tess? You got me good and proper.' His head nodded up and down a few times. 'I didn't see that one coming, though I should have.'

'I was never your girlfriend, Cody.' Jean spat her words out.

Prince played on; he played on and on beneath them, even though the party was over. Jonti shook his head, like he was an old man with a tremor. Lewis watched the hand on the gun. Toby stood, nose pointed straight at Cody and Benny, watching too. A gun dog who knows gun is master.

Finally, Tess said, 'I don't see with your eyes, Benny. I told you that before.'

'Just as well, cause I can't see a fucking thing out this eye now, can I!' His voice was raw and hollow.

Jean, fight ready always, growled at her side. 'Who the fuck are you?'

'No, who the fuck are *you*?' said Benny.

'I'm her girlfriend, you fuck-head. And don't come into my house uninvited and ask me to explain myself.'

'You telling me you're a fucking lezzo now, Tess?'

Tess couldn't move, she couldn't speak. The shadow over Ben had pressure that welded her to the ground, shut tight her mouth, froze her muscles, her thoughts. But still she could see, she could see his rage at being stolen from and lied to, at being left alone. He turned it on them now, cold stones.

'No,' said Jonti. 'No, no, no.'

'Cody, please leave,' said Jean. 'Both of you get out of my house. You're freaking out my brother.'

'Your brother is a freak. He always was,' said Cody. Then he shook his head. 'You owe me, Jean.'

'I am not,' said Jonti. 'No, no, no.'

'You can have money. You can have anything in this house, apart from the people. Just take what you want and get the fuck away.'

How steely Jean was, how sure she pretended to be, though Tess could see she was also terrified.

Still Cody shook his head. 'It's not what I meant. You're a cock-tease. You can't do that to me, you can't make like you want it and not take it.'

'Don't you talk to my daughter like that, you creep.' Lewis

was angry. 'And who are you?' He pointed at Benny.

'Yeah, go on,' said Benny. 'Tell them who I am.'

Tess was silent.

'All righty, then I'll tell you. Tess is *my* girlfriend. I haven't seen her in a while, and she owes me something.' He raised his eyebrows, pretended to look around. 'Nice wee set-up you got here, Tess. But easy come, easy go, eh . . .'

Tess's legs were shaking, and she felt Jean pull slightly away from her.

'You shouldn't have left like that, Tess. So quickly, not even saying goodbye. Do your new friends here know what you did?'

Tess couldn't look at them but she could feel their eyes, Anne, Lewis, Jean and Jonti, hard on her.

Benny laughed. 'When Cody here told me you two were lezzos, I didn't believe him.' He breathed out heavy. 'But it's true, eh.'

His eyes were confused and blank, so blank. There was no way she could pull him out from that place, but she tried. She watched him with as much care as she could summon.

He flashed. 'Don't fucking stare at me, Tess, don't you fucking try and pull my brain out of my head.'

'You're cracked in the head,' said Jean.

'Shut up, bitch!' said Benny.

'What did you do, Tess?' said Jean. For once she sounded afraid.

'No no no no,' said Jonti.

'What did you do?' Jean shouted.

Tess could see now—she should have told Jean, she should have told Jean who she was, what she could do, what she had done.

'And you!' Jean pointed at Benny. 'You're such a big man,

aren't you. So big, walking in here with my dad's gun and your big talk. Just get the fuck out of here.'

'Jean!' said Tess. She felt that Jean had no stop button, and now Benny turned his emptiness on her.

'What do you know?' he said, his chin bullish, stepping towards her. 'What the fuck do you know about what this bitch can do?'

There was sweat on Benny's forehead now, beading and running down his temple. It was a part of him she'd found attractive, his temple, the soft skin with delicate veins beneath.

'She can see into your brain, she can see the shit you don't want to see yourself. She's a witch, she's fucking mental, and she'll make you mental too.'

'Benny . . .' Tess's voice was despair. She didn't love him, she knew that, but neither did she want to see him like this.

'Tess,' said Jean quietly. 'What's going on here?'

Tess looked at her. If only she could show Jean, show Jean in pictures everything that was running through her own head. Doug's leg, Rose's strung-out face, the soggy loaf of bread, Jonti's trapped birds, a horse named Moss that she'd never met, a black pot on a ring of fire. Somehow these things made sense in Tess's head. They were the quickest way of explaining herself and the world around her, the clear, desperate love she needed to prove to Jean. Jean.

And with that Tess moved—thought shaped lightning quick. She knew she couldn't wrestle the gun off Cody, he was too strong, but she was fast and she had her ring, and again she struck him, this time in the neck, missing the artery, although she knew the instant she saw the surface blood run down that she'd meant to go for it and she'd missed.

Cody was fast too, though this time Lewis was faster. From

the corner of her eye she saw him dive, throwing his whole body on Cody, wrestling him to the ground. Anne following to pin Cody down, Benny moving to help Cody, and then, Tess did not know how, Jean had the rifle and it fired, and Benny was down too.

He let out an animal howl, and Tess turned, momentarily thinking Jean was hurt, that Jean had been shot. But she hadn't been. Jean was okay. Jean was lowering the rifle from her burning eye and there was no pleasure, no victory, but a grim satisfaction in hitting her target, in maiming the man who meant her family harm.

Benny doubled over.

'Fuck, fuck!' He shouted out his pain over and over, and Tess saw the blood soaking his light canvas shoe.

'You shot him, Jean!' Jonti was shouting. 'You shot him!'

'Your foot?' Tess made to move to him, to help.

'Leave him!' said Jean. 'He's a piece of shit.' And Tess did as Jean said.

Jean raised the rifle again and pointed it at Cody. 'Anne, go and call the ambulance, call the cops, and if any of you fuckwits move, I'll shoot you. Stay on him, Lewis.'

Anne left the room and Toby sat by his mistress while she pointed the rifle at the two young men. Everyone was breathing hard, as if all of them had run a race, and Benny was giving out a low whimper as the pain pulsed through his shot foot. There was blood all over the carpet and Prince was still playing and Jonti kept saying, *You did it this time, Jean, you shot him, not me. You did it this time.* Over and over, until Jean said, *Yes, Jonti, I shot him, it was me, not you, never you.*

It was four in the morning when Jean got back from the police station. The cops were having a busy night and they told Lewis to take her home.

Tess was in Jean's seat on the deck. She stood up and Jean stood below her, one foot on the step. Lewis raised a heavy brow at Tess and walked into the house, leaving the two of them alone.

An early bird called out; light was coming into the sky. Tess felt like her eyeballs were going to crack.

'Jean,' she said.

Jean was looking out to the garden. When she turned back, her face was too hard for Tess to look at, and Tess blinked, as though there was something caught in her eye. She felt that she couldn't take in enough air, her stomach and chest were clamped.

'You know, the whole time I was at the cop shop and they were questioning me, I was thinking how for so long I've thought my family were these terrible people who kept secrets, and here it turns out that you're worse than us.' Jean's voice was very calm. She spoke in quiet, measured tones. 'Lewis told me what he knew about you. He told me what you told him you can do, and I sat there trying to work why you'd told him and not me. And what this means about how you really feel about me. Because if you told Benny what you can do, and you told Lewis what you can do, but you didn't tell me, I don't know you. I don't know who you are.'

Now Tess realised the calm wasn't something Jean was

controlling. It was more that she was speaking from behind a closed door. Trust misplaced.

Tess was silent. There were words she wanted to say bubbling in her. They burst when she tried to form them into meaning.

'It's a curse. What I have,' she said. Sheila had said that once, *Our cursed family*. 'You heard what Benny did with it. It doesn't help anyone if they know.'

'Lewis knew. Because you told him.' Jean's voice was hurt now, accusing.

'I didn't plan to, Jean. It just came out because . . . Because Lewis tried to kiss me and I saw that woman he was with when your mum died. She was in his eyes. He still loves her.'

'Lewis kissed you?'

'Well, he tried, but no. I mean, gross.'

'Why are you telling me this now?'

'It was before I met you, and nothing happened. It was nothing.'

Jean looked at her, weighing Tess with her hard internal measure. And she gave in. She shook her head and said, 'Fuck you, Tess, you should have told me. You should have told me everything.' Then she went quiet. Toby padded out to her, and Jean said, 'Hello, boy. Happy New Year.' She looked at Tess. 'All I want to know is—what have you seen in me?'

Tess answered slowly, carefully. 'Someone I want to be with.'

Jean's anger flashed out. 'What does that mean?'

'All I see in you, Jean, is what you show me. That's all I can do. And what I see, I like. I love.'

Frail Jean, tough Jean, Jean who knew how to use a rifle when she needed to. Jean who demanded the truth.

'So, tell me. What have you seen?' she said.

Tess moved away off the deck and down the steps and stood

by Jean a minute. She reached out her hand and waited for Jean to take it. Jean shook her head, so Tess said, 'At least sit down?' and Jean did.

'It wasn't an accident, was it?' said Tess. 'Jonti meant to shoot your mum, didn't he?' She didn't look at Jean. She wanted to hear her answer, not see it.

She felt Jean turn away, her instinctive reaction to deny knowledge. But Tess was patient. She held her hands together as if praying, willing Jean to believe that she was safe.

When Jean finally spoke, her tone was strange. Quiet, unsteady. 'Yeah,' she said. 'He did.'

So now Tess looked at her and Jean looked back, and Tess could see it clearly—Alan bent over Hannah's prone, damaged body, shouting at Jean, Jonti backing away with the hunting rifle still in his hands, his whole body shaking.

Tess leaned forwards and nudged Jean with her head, and Jean whispered, her voice low because she couldn't bear to speak out loud, 'He was trying to protect me.'

'From what?' whispered Tess.

'From her.'

'From Hannah?'

Jean breathed hard and nodded.

'She scared him. I never understood why, but Mum and Jonti . . . It's like she couldn't see how funny he could be, how good his weirdness is. She was always ashamed of him. She wanted a perfect family. And we weren't. Me and Jonti never were quite good enough for her.'

'What happened?' said Tess.

'We'd had a fight over a dress of hers I wanted to wear. She had nice clothes. She wouldn't let me borrow it, so I just took it. I was trying it on in my room and she just walked in and started trying to pull it off me. She told me I was too fat to wear it. And we started yelling, calling each other names. I ran out and she ran after me, and she got hold of the hem, ripping at it, and I don't know . . . Jonti, he went to the garage and he got Dad's hunting rifle. I guess he meant to frighten her.' She paused. 'Actually, I don't know what he meant. But he shot her, he shot our mum.' Jean touched her head, where the bullet had gone in. 'It was a bad shot, he was always a bad shot, or maybe he meant it that way.' She shrugged. Then she looked hard at Tess and she was so undone that Tess wanted to cry and hold her, but instead Tess held herself. Jean needed her steady.

Jean said, 'Do you know?'

Tess thought about Jonti, how she'd looked away from what he'd shown her the first time they met. Perhaps she'd known since then. She'd seen his grief and his fear and his confusion, the birds and animals that ran wild in his mind and that he tried to set free in the grass. It wasn't clear to Tess what he'd meant to do. It wasn't that simple. There was no clear way to tell the past, just as there was no clear way to see what was coming. She might see other people's memories but they weren't hers. She shook her head.

'No,' said Tess. 'I don't.'

They were quiet for a moment, then Jean continued.

'Alan and Lewis had him sectioned instead of going through court. They lied about it. It was Alan and Lewis who said it was an accident.'

Tess hugged her then, and Jean dug her head into Tess's shoulder. 'I'm supposed to be grateful for that, but I can't be.'

'No.'

'I miss him, Tess. I miss my brother.'

*

Tess walked Jean through to her room, pulled the covers up and sat by her, stroking her hair from her forehead. She watched Jean's eyes open and close, open and close. She sat by her, hand on her arm, until her breathing deepened and she was certain Jean was asleep. She leaned over and kissed her on the forehead. *Goodbye*, she whispered. *I love you.*

In the living room Lewis was sitting with Anne, talking quietly. He said he'd taken Jonti back to the unit, and the cops had called. They said Benny might lose his foot, and wanted Tess and Jean to come in tomorrow for further questioning. Tess nodded and said, *I'm sorry, Lewis, I'm so sorry.* And Lewis sighed and said, *I know, Tess. I know.* His face was grave, dark hollows under his eyes.

Tess sat down on Jonti's bed, alone. She was exhausted. Her brain flashed neon lights in her eyes, and it hurt. She didn't know how to begin to explain Benny to the cops. She could say he was jealous, she could bargain on the hope that he wouldn't talk about Doug, about the money. But she didn't want to lie anymore, she was too tired. All she could think to do was run from Benny, from the cops, from explaining it all to Jean, but most especially from herself.

Don't run away from my daughter, Lewis had said. But she couldn't help what she was.

Alan had been at the hospital, discharging the young woman who'd had her stomach pumped, only fourteen. These kids, the drinking they did. Plus he'd been back and forth with a young man who would most likely lose a foot from a breaking and entering that had gone wrong. He'd been shot. Alan didn't know the full story, didn't want to know. There was a limit to the stories he could hold in his head, a limit to the caring he could do. He shook his head at the waste of it, and then, perhaps because of his tiredness, as he placed his key in the ignition of his car he allowed himself to remember Hannah. Sometimes, in the darkest hours of night, he allowed himself to remember holding her, after they'd made love. He'd thought he'd have longer with her than those brief moments, perhaps the rest of their lives, but he didn't. And then it hit him. *I am just like those kids*, he thought. I too have pushed. I too have been toppled.

As he pulled out of the hospital to drive home, he didn't see the young woman on the other side of the road, her thumb raised to hitch a lift. Through the haze of remembering what had been lost, he didn't see Tess, her pack on her back, thin frame, stringy hair, her face flashing between defiance and grief. He did not see the car pull over for her, the car she would get inside and be taken away in, far out of town.

ACKNOWLEDGEMENTS

I am exceptionally grateful to the Louis Johnson Estate and Creative New Zealand for the 2013 Creative New Zealand Louis Johnson Emerging Writers Bursary.

An enormous thank you to—

My colleagues at VUP: Fergus Barrowman, Ashleigh Young, Holly Hunter, Craig Gamble and Kyleigh Hodgson, for their encouragement and conversation and for pretending to let me boss them around.

Jane Parkin for her brilliant editing skills and care.

Keely O'Shannessy for the magnificent cover.

My old friends Sarah Graydon, Heyden O'Brien and Jonah Marinovich—the coolest kids in town.

David Long, whose love and support is a gift.

This book is dedicated to my sisters.